THROWAWAYS

A Jake Savage Mystery

Elliott D. Light

COPYRIGHT

THROWAWAYS
Copyright © 2020 Elliott D. Light
ISBN: 978-1-61088-528-7 (paperback)
ISBN: 978-1-61088-529-4 (ebook)
ISBN: 978-1-61088-530-0 (audiobook)
All rights reserved

Published by Bancroft Press ("Books that Enlighten")
P.O. Box 65360, Baltimore, MD 21209
Phone: 800-637-7377
Fax: 410-764-1967
Email: bruceb@bancroftpress.com
www.bancroftpress.com

Also visit www.elliottlight.com for more information

Cover art, book formatting and author photo editing by
Anita Dugan-Moore of Cyber Bytz, www.cyber-bytz.com

Author photo by John F. Morgan, John Morgan Photography,
www.jfmorgan.com

bancroft
press

IN MEMORY OF TSUKI

My friend, my muse, and my enigmatic companion, Tsuki, was the consummate feline, an expert at practiced indifference who made me smile every day. I miss her.

ACKNOWLEDGMENTS

I view this section of a book as a slippery slope. Letting folks know that their support is appreciated is a noble undertaking. The danger is that once you start, you may leave someone unrecognized.

That said, at the top of the list is my friend and spouse, Sonya. Without her patience, understanding and high standards, this book would never have been finished.

I have been blessed with great support from my publisher, Bruce Bortz, and the patient guiding hand of Anita Moore, whose cover graphic pops with enthusiasm. Anita's steady guidance as to the workings of the evolving book distribution and marketing world have been invaluable.

So much to be grateful for.

Elliott

CONTENTS

PREVIEW - THE GENE POLICE

DAY 1

SUNDAY, OCTOBER 18, 2019

CHAPTER ONE

A young girl's body drifted over the reef where I was scuba diving. Had it not been for the shadow cast by the body, I might not have looked up.

Just moments earlier, I'd been hovering beneath the surface of the warm Gulf water off Key West, enthralled by what nature had brought me. Highlighted by a ray of sunlight, a lionfish, a beautiful brown-striped creature with feathery pectoral fins and venomous spines, bobbed in the gentle current, watching me. This particular fish wasn't just a curiosity, but an invasive species that was not only threatening the Florida ecosystem but the waters of the Caribbean and northward into Georgia.

Through no fault of its own, the lionfish had become a top predator, eating much of the food once shared by the indigenous marine life and upsetting the fragile balance of the local ecosystem. As a research volunteer with ClearSeas, I was tasked with counting these invaders, photographing them, and uploading my information to a database.

Before I could frame the fish properly, the sunlight illuminating its ethereal beauty dimmed, the rays lost to a shadow of unknown origin that seemed to be moving with the current. I looked up and found the shadow's source. An object floating on the surface had drifted over the reef where I was diving. For a moment, I was curious, transfixed, the shock of its sudden appearance having slowed the processing of what I was looking at.

Understanding gave way to horror. Adrenaline flooded my head. My heartbeat sounded like thunder; I was sucking air from my regulator but couldn't catch my breath. Despite the impulse to deny what I was seeing, I slowly realized that my photographic session with a lionfish had been interrupted by the body of a young girl floating face down in the water. Her hair had fanned out in a halo of sorts, undulating gently on the surface. For an instant, I thought — or hoped — she might be watching me, but she had no snorkel or mask. She wasn't wearing a swimsuit, either, but was clad in only a shirt and panties. As I came closer, I realized she couldn't have looked at me because she had no eyes. *She had no eyes!*

Continuing its trek eastward, her body drifted past me and the sun returned. I didn't want to go to her, to see what I knew were the tortured remains of a once living human being. I had seen ravaged bodies up close and dreaded the idea of seeing hers. I wanted her to leave. I wanted her to disappear. If I just waited a few minutes, she would be out of my sight, a tiny speck in the vast Gulf waters. A voice pleaded with me to let her go, but despite being repulsed by the condition of her face, I simply couldn't leave her to the whims of the wind and tide. She deserved better.

Approaching her from underneath, I held my breath to avoid hitting her with my bubbles. I stopped a few feet below her but avoided looking directly at her. To calm myself, I tried to imagine her alive, what she might say, the sound of her voice, the story she might tell me. "How," I would ask, "did you arrive at this place? Where is your family? What events conspired to take your life? Are you cold? What am I supposed to do? How did you find me? Why me?"

Even if alive, the girl who had momentarily blocked the sun might have refused to answer my questions. She didn't know me. She wouldn't understand the reasons her story was so important to me or why and how we were now connected. If she'd asked, I don't know that I could have told her.

Swimming past her, I turned and grabbed the collar of her blouse and slowly guided her to my anchor rope, securing her with string from my collection bag.

On board my boat, I fumbled with my phone, finally steadying my hands sufficiently to call the police. The dispatcher was calm to the point of indifference.

"You said your name is Jake Savage and you live on Raccoon Key?"

"That's my name. I live in Old Town, but the boat is registered to my mother, who lives on Raccoon Key."

"Your mother is Ethel Savage?"

"Yes. My adopted mother."

"Are you a minor? Adult?"

"Adult."

"Age?"

"I'm twenty-seven."

"Ok. So, you found a body in the water? Is that why you're calling?"

"Yes, goddamn it. That's what I said."

"Please, sir. I'm just trying to confirm the facts. A dead body?"

"Yes. I've secured her to my boat. You need to send a recovery crew."

"The victim is female?"

"Yes."

"Are you related?"

"What? No. I said I found her while diving."

"Was there an accident?"

"No. I don't know. What's wrong with you? I said I found her at the GPS coordinates I gave you. I don't know her or where she came from or anything about her. Someone needs to come and recover her body. That's why I'm calling."

"It's important to remain calm. Okay? Let me see what I can do. Things are kind of crazy here because of Fantasy Fest. I'm sure you can understand how busy we are with festival week."

"She has no eyes," saying out loud a thought that just popped into my head.

"Who...what...?

"The body I found. She had no eyes. Why would that be?"

I heard a sigh. "I don't know, Jake. Fish maybe? Try not to think about that right now. I'll get someone out there as quickly as I can."

I sat on the bench at the aft of the boat watching clouds building in the west. I did my best to think about nothing, grimacing away the images of the dead girl that forced their way into my thoughts.

I have no idea how long it was before I saw flashing blue and red lights approaching. The police boat pulled next to mine. A young officer started to question me, then realized we had attended high school together.

"You don't remember me. I'm Freddy Squires. I was the bench gofer for the varsity basketball team your senior year. You were pretty good."

"Not really. At six-three, I was too short to be a forward and too slow to be a guard. I could shoot, but that's about it."

Revisiting our high school days a few feet from a dead child struck me as surreal. I glanced at the anchor rope, thinking that we should be helping her, not revisiting the long-forgotten days when we were her age. But the questions continued. Freddy was thorough and trained to consider every person involved in an incident as a suspect — even a former classmate. His suspicions addressed, he entered the water with a marine body bag and a camera.

After a few minutes, he popped to the surface and handed his camera to me. "Batteries are dead. I'm afraid that with this current getting her into a body bag is a two-person job."

The thought of seeing her again wrapped me in dread, so much so that for a moment I didn't move.

"I'm sorry, Jake. There's a storm coming so we have to hurry."

I returned to the water. Freddy pointed to places on her body he wanted photographed — marks on her neck, shoulders, and thighs. Together, we positioned the body bag around the young girl and secured it with straps. A few minutes later, she was on board the police boat. I transferred the photos from my camera to the officer's laptop, returned to my boat, and watched as Freddy and the remains of the young girl headed back to Key West.

The return ride to Raccoon Key was challenging. The normally flat waters had begun to churn because of wind-driven rain, tossing my small boat like a cork and actually bringing the engine briefly out of the water. Once inside the key, the waters calmed even as the rain fell in torrents. I eased the boat into its slip,

5

tied it off, and sat under the canopy as rain fell around and on me. Looking toward the house, I saw Ethy standing under the eaves of the second story balcony. She watched me for moment before turning away and disappearing inside.

Despite being wet and exhausted, I was reluctant to join her. Ethy was a worrier. But rather than addressing the source of her angst, she would lash out at those who made her fret. Today, because of the storm, because I was late, that would be me. At least for the moment, I was better off on the boat.

My relationship with Ethel Savage is complicated, primarily because she isn't my biological mother and because she often reminded me of that fact while growing up. I came to live with her and Maurice Savage when I was four, just after my mother died. Maurice and Ethel owned the bar where my mother worked. Maurice loved me like one of his own and was the force behind my adoption. Ethel went along with the idea but was never warm or welcoming. As a child, I referred to Maurice as "Pop" and Ethel as "Ethy." I still call her by that name, despite her protestations, or maybe because of them.

Things became even more complicated a few months back when Ethy had a mild stroke. The rehab facility where she was treated wouldn't release her to her home unless someone was there to keep an eye on her. Her biological son was in prison for murder and her biological daughter was living in Orlando with a man who had three kids. Having finished college and grad school, I was self-employed, specializing in the statistical analysis of complex systems. Ethy equated self-employment with unemployment and insisted I was the ideal candidate to provide her care.

Realistically, Ethy could afford to pay someone to stay with her. While Maurice had made a lot of bad choices during his long business life, buying and selling real estate wasn't one of them.

He'd sold the bar in old town Key West for a substantial gain, invested in property out of town, and built the two-story house on the water where Ethy now lived. A trust fund would have provided the money for Ethy's care, but Ethy insisted she would rather be dead than cared for by strangers. The crying, self-pity, and theatrics about being unloved in her time of need took their toll on my better judgment, so I agreed to play the role of guardian.

After a month, it was clear to me that living with Ethy would drive us both mad. I placed an ad for someone to take my place in exchange for free rent. After sorting through dozens of responses, I interviewed Tess Simpson. A twenty-something woman with a degree in history, she had grown up as a military brat who traveled to places I couldn't find on a map. She was assertive without being aggressive and exuded a confidence I found comforting. I'll admit that, before entrusting Ethy's care to her, I should have asked more questions, particularly about what she was doing in the Keys. But Tess was just so likable, and I was so desperate to get out of the house, that I offered her the job on the spot. She was also very pretty.

To my relief, Ethy agreed to give her a try. I agreed to stay in Key West, which is just a few miles away, while Ethy and Tess became better acquainted. I moved into a small ramshackle house left to me by my biological mother and decided to spend Tess' trial period renovating it. Tess turned out to have the patience of a stone requiring me to handle smaller doses of Ethy's passive-aggressive behavior. Gradually, I found a balance between my obligations to her and my desire to renovate the bungalow where I had spent the first four years of my life.

The rain ended as quickly as it began. I gathered my camera and wet towel and headed to Ethy's place. When I stepped inside, Ethy was seated in front of the television. She spoke without looking at me, first complaining that Tess was late, then insisting

7

that I put my wet things in the laundry and, last but not least, warning me not to clean the fish in the kitchen because it always smelled bad afterwards. "Maurice would never listen. You're just like him."

When I told her I had caught no fish, she shouted something about wasting my time on her boat. I promised to make something later for dinner and went outside to the lanai, a beer in hand, to watch the sunset and to clear my head of the image of the dead girl with no eyes.

Sergeant Detective Trent Murphy arrived an hour later. I heard him talking to Ethy. She was asking whether I was in trouble, and from there commented on how I spent so much time on her boat, how hard it was for her, having just had a small stroke, but how easy it was for me, because I was tall and good at sports, even though I didn't really practice much. She even mentioned I had a photographic memory, which gave me an advantage on tests. *Blah blah blah.*

When she saw I was listening to her, she made sure I knew I had pissed her off.

"Then he gets a couple a college diplomas, comes here, and struts around like one of those island roosters. He doesn't have a job other than fixing boats and working on that old house his mother left him. Sometimes he looks for treasure, just like my dead husband Maurice did. Lot of good college did for Jake, or anyone for that matter."

What Ethy didn't mention was that I had turned down a job offer from ClearSeas as head of statistical analysis in order to take care of her. I saw no reason to remind her.

"Jake's outside," she continued. "I don't know if he'll talk to you without an appointment."

The detective stepped out onto the lanai and introduced himself. He took a seat opposite me, took out a notepad and a small pencil, and sighed loudly.

My memory is conditioned to make observations and imprint information quickly. Detective Murphy was in his late fifties or early sixties. His face wasn't so much wrinkled as defined by creases, pockmarks, and the subtle development of jowls and a small wattle under his chin. His gray hair was receding, leaving a large space between his eyes and his new hairline. His right eye was noticeably higher than the left.

Impressions are what happen when information is filtered through lenses of experience, bias and, to some extent, wishful thinking. First impressions tend to be lasting because they are, well, first. Besides being tired, Detective Murphy struck me as a sad man, or more precisely, a man who rarely experienced joy. He exuded a vibe of indifference, a man going through the motions of a job that frustrated him.

What Detective Murphy couldn't know was that before he said or did anything, I was inclined to distrust him. I had plenty of experience with police investigators — repeatedly attempting to get them to reopen my mother's murder case, pressing for new forensic testing of old evidence, mining new state DNA databases, whether legal or not, and using genealogy to link crime DNA to relatives in hopes of finding a suspect.

While I might have been more tactful, all the various police explanations for not pursuing the case had one big thing in common — the belief that it wasn't worth expending police resources to solve an old case when other more recent crimes needed attention. Fair or not, I construed this to mean that my mother's life wasn't worth bothering with.

Against this bias, Detective Murphy sat in front of me, fulfilling the obligations of his job with all the enthusiasm of a man who mopped floors for a living.

He introduced himself again, then said: "Thank you for helping to recover the body and for photographing it. As the first person on the scene, I need to hear from you directly how you came to find the body, if you know who the young girl is, and how you tied her to the anchor rope. The details matter."

I related what I saw and what I did, then asked what would be done to identify her.

"If she's not local or on a missing persons list, the odds of learning who she was diminish significantly. The officer you met seems to think it was an accident. We get transients and runaways down here all the time who pay to go on a party boat cruise. Sometimes they get loaded and fall off, but usually no one drowns. At least, no one reports it because of possible drug usage. Besides, party boat operators don't like cops."

Whatever the detective meant, what I heard was that the victim's social status mattered, reminding me what had been said or implied about my mother.

"Is there a department that specializes in crimes against transients?" I asked.

Ethy soon joined us on the lanai, stood by the detective, and stared at me, fear in her eyes. "I don't think Detective Murphy meant anything like that."

The detective glanced at us, puzzled, unaware of the live wire he'd almost stepped on.

Looking to reassure Ethy that I wasn't going to verbally assault the detective, I smiled at her. "I'm sure he didn't."

"You don't think it was an accident?" he asked.

I said I didn't and went through my reasoning: "her blouse wasn't buttoned correctly, and her panties were on backwards. She wore no jewelry, despite having pierced ears. Her makeup looked fresh despite a lot of time spent in the water, suggesting she could afford expensive, waterproof products. Marks on her shoulders and thighs suggested she was assaulted. Most notably, she had a rather elaborate tattoo of a butterfly on her left thigh. Tattoos like that cost a lot of money."

Detective Murphy made notes, then cautioned me against jumping to conclusions. He assured me he would look at the crime photos and the Medical Examiner's report and do what needed to be done. He was adamant that it was a police matter and would be handled properly. I agreed, without much conviction, that he would do all he could.

When he left, Ethy uncharacteristically gave me a sympathetic look. "You saw a… body?"

I nodded. "A young girl. She'd been desecrated by fish and crabs, but she looked to be a teenager."

"You took pictures?"

"The camera on the police boat wasn't working. It's no big deal. Really. I mean, you heard the detective. The police will handle it. Anyway, I didn't have time to spear any lionfish. After I finish my beer, I'll make dinner."

"I think we should do carryout," she said. "Let's do pizza. My treat."

Tess arrived just after I came home with the pizza and beer. She apologized for being late, talked about the storm, and accepted an invitation to join us for dinner. Ethy and I let her talk,

11

acknowledging her comments with nods and smiles, but otherwise ate and drank without speaking.

While cleaning up, Tess took me aside.

"Are you okay?"

I shrugged. "Yeah. Why do you ask?"

"I don't know, maybe because Ethy wasn't picking on you and you weren't looking at your watch?"

I shook my head. "We're good."

Ethy appeared in the kitchen with a plate of leftover pizza. "Jake found a body today," she said, "and a police detective came by to question him. The cops think it was an accident, but Jake seems to think otherwise. Jake's really good with details."

For a moment, Tess seemed stunned.

I was too. It did indeed sound as if Ethy was bragging on me.

Tess stepped in front of me on her way to the dishwasher. "Curious what passes for good with you."

I stepped around her and put the empty beer bottles in the recycling bin.

"How did the girl die?" asked Tess.

I shrugged. "Hard to say. I think the operating theory is that it was an accident. She drank too much and fell off a boat. For reasons no one can explain, no one reported her missing."

"Of course, you think it was something else."

I looked at Ethy. "What I think doesn't matter."

Tess started to speak, but Ethy shushed her with a shake of her head.

I took the leftover pizza slices and headed home.

CHAPTER TWO

My house in Key West is in a neighborhood of small block homes, bungalows and clapboard cottages referred to as Cayman Village. Some of these residences were restored; others were decidedly in disrepair. To an untrained eye, they simply looked old and cramped, a thousand square feet or less of living space, typically with two bedrooms and a single bath. But this was island living where space was at a premium. For decades, families lived here, working hard to provide food, drink, and cleaning services to the seasonal snowbirds who flocked to the island every fall and departed in the spring.

My mother, Gretchen Favor, acquired this house from her parents and then left it to me. Maurice managed it on my behalf, renting it, repairing it, and keeping it livable. After he died, the house was all but forgotten. The trustee who managed Ethy's money continued to pay the property taxes, as Maurice had directed, but no one bothered with maintenance, and for the last few years, the house remained unoccupied, at least by anyone paying rent.

When I returned to Key West to take care of Ethy, I found the property overgrown and the house infested by rodents and an assortment of Florida's largest insects. Using plywood, I covered a few broken windows and tried to remove the colonies of mold flourishing in the rain-soaked drywall below them. Several bottles of bleach later, I realized that making the house livable again would require a full renovation.

One day, I woke up, and being more than a little impulsive, took a two-pound hammer and went to work removing walls, baseboard, and bathroom fixtures. I was a human tornado. Only the kitchen, a toilet, and a shower escaped destruction. Unfortunately, I later realized how much easier it was to demolish a house than to put it back together.

I left Ethy's house and arrived at my cottage just after nine. Sitting on the porch with a beer and a bag of chips, I did my best to avoid thinking about the dead girl and Detective Murphy's honest but infuriating explanation of how the girl's death would probably remain unexplained. Of course, by trying not to think about these things, they quickly occupied my mind. I countered by reminding myself that the dead girl wasn't my problem to solve. The problem belonged to Detective Murphy and the Key West police, neither of which seemed to give a damn about figuring out who she was or what had happened to her.

I wasted a beer on this exercise, finally deciding that my time was best spent sanding drywall, an impulse that lasted only few minutes. With little accomplished and no motivation to tackle anything else, I headed for bed.

An instant after I flicked the bedroom light switch, the lightbulb exploded in a shower of sparks and glass fragments. With the aid of a flashlight, the reason for the pyrotechnic display became apparent: the light fixture was nearly full of water. Closer inspection revealed a brown stain on the ceiling surrounding the fixture, and a puddle on the floor below it. The storm that had swamped the boat had exploited a void, pushing water into the attic space above my room. With rain likely every afternoon, the problem couldn't be ignored.

I fetched a bucket, caulk, sealing tape, and a trash bag and pulled down the ladder that led to the attic. I gripped that ladder and stared into the dark rectangle above me. "Why does every fucking thing have to be so hard?" I thought.

I was gripped by an irrational but palatable fear of dark spaces, particularly those that were playgrounds for bats, rats, and spiders. I scolded myself for being frightened of the dark, screamed a loud "shit" and forged ahead.

Popping my head into the attic, I was met by a cloud of hot, humid air heavy with the scent of wet wood and urine. I panned the dark space with the flashlight, its narrow beam catching the remains of old chairs, broken mirrors, a highchair, and a pile of old carpets. Closer to the entrance, the floor was littered with mice droppings and shredded paper. Seeing no eyes staring back at me, I stepped into the attic, located a light bulb hanging from a wire and, before turning it on, slapped the socket to make sure it wasn't electrically hot.

Even in the dim light, I could see multiple stains in the plywood sheathing that formed the roof. On the front side of the roof, a section of plywood had partially collapsed. Above my bedroom, water had darkened a large area of sheathing and was still dripping.

In order to get a clear view of the leak, I needed to move a pile of old furniture covered in spider webs and mouse feces. Bracing for a swarm of mice and angry palmetto bugs, I slid the old carpet to one side and then started with the furniture. Underneath an old wicker rocking chair was a small wooden box, the word "MEMENTOS" barely visible in faded red ink. I retrieved the box but thought better of opening it. Placing it aside, I focused the flashlight's beam on the ceiling's wet area. A few minutes of poking and pressing made it clear that patching the leak from the inside would be futile. I placed the bucket under the drip, grabbed the box, turned off the light, and climbed down the ladder.

I took a long shower, which left me clean but wide awake. In the kitchen, I sprayed the wooden box with a disinfecting cleaner, then wiped it dry with a paper towel. After covering the kitchen table with newspaper, I set the box down and opened it. I'll admit to briefly entertaining fantasies of finding something remarkable in the box — perhaps a stash of gold coins or a map to an old pirate's treasure. The fantasies faded quickly when I gazed upon a mass of faded, cracked, and disintegrating photographs. I tried to pick up one photo that appeared to be intact, but it quickly crumbled into dozens of small fragments.

Under the photographs was a small stack of yellowed paper held together by a rusted staple. Even before I pulled the papers free of the box, I knew they were printouts of emails. Another minute passed before I realized I had discovered an actual treasure — something that gave me chills and made my heart race.

I was looking at an email exchange between my mother, "KWGretchen," and someone identified as "KWJames."

I handled the papers carefully, almost reverently, looking at them more than reading them. The messages spanned a week or so in January, eight months before I was born. Attached to the last page was an opened letter postmarked a few months before my mother's death.

I had vague memories of my mother — fragments of images of her smile and her eyes. What had stuck with me was her voice, a soothing and comforting sound that talked me to sleep before she

16

went to work and lulled me from bed when it was time to get up. I could hear her laugh when we were being silly which was often but never enough. As I read her emails, I could hear her, conversing with the man I was certain was my dad. I had never heard his voice, but I could imagine it from the way he talked to my mother.

The thread of emails started with a congratulatory message from James.

> "If you are reading this, then you have successfully logged into the email account I created for you. Now we can communicate wherever I'm stationed. I miss you! Know that once I'm out of the navy, we will be together forever. Write me back!!"

The emails that followed were of the same ilk: two young people separated by time and space clinging to each other, an exchange of words intended for their eyes only. The messages captured expressions of passion and intimate thoughts sprinkled with the mundane: "I can't wait to kiss you, to touch you." "It rained today." "I couldn't find my keys." "A man left me a twenty-dollar tip because I talked to him about his dying wife." "The computer at the bar quit working." "I want you to hold me."

But the warm and loving thoughts came to an end, terminated by an email from my mother that was blunt and intended to be so:

> "I have enjoyed the last few months with you more than I can say, but you have to understand that you have no future with me. There is so much you don't know about me, so much I can't tell you. I beg you to leave me alone and to move on."

The message seemed to come out of the blue, a "Dear John" delivered without any provocation. Perhaps there were other messages that would explain my mother's change of heart, but if there were, they weren't saved.

The last item was a letter dated four years later, and a month before my mother was murdered:

> "Dear Gretchen:
>
> I'm not sure if you will receive this letter or read it if you do. I am coming to Key West for a conference and would like to see you, to talk to you about what happened so long ago. Please let me know if that is something you would be willing to do, and we can set up a time and place. I will understand if you decide not to see me but want you to know I've never stopped thinking about you or caring about you.
>
> — James"

I took the emails and a beer and sat on the porch. It was after midnight. Crickets serenaded an empty street as a light breeze rustled the palm trees. A few hours earlier, I had sat here, my thoughts spinning around the death of a young girl. Here I was again, this time trying to grasp the significance of a handful of old emails and a letter that may never have been answered. Objectively, the emails changed nothing. My mother was still dead, and her killer still unknown. I had a pretty good idea of the first name of my father, but so what? The most definitive piece of information was that my mother had ended the relationship, but that knowledge also had no apparent utility. The timing of the letter — just before my mother was killed — was interesting but not meaningful.

Useful or otherwise, I gazed at the faded paper, taking solace in having something my mother had touched. I heard her voice, felt her hand on my face. Tears flooded my eyes, and I let them come.

I was gripped by a familiar hollow feeling, an immense sadness that lives in the shadows of conscious thought, a feeling born out of an intense longing for someone who died decades ago and died again yesterday. I let myself sob and shake until the memory of that someone retreated, and the pain subsided. Exhausted, I headed back to my room, stepped around the broken light bulb, and fell into bed, shoes and all.

DAY 2

MONDAY, OCTOBER 19

CHAPTER THREE

Sleep proved an ineffective refuge. The night was spent dreaming of a floating body, my murdered mom, and a boatload of dead people I'd encountered as a teenager.

When the morning came, I was exhausted but relieved to be free of the images served up by my overly creative subconscious. Gathering paper, pen, and a cup of coffee, I sat at the kitchen table and made a list of the day's projects and the things I needed from Home Depot to accomplish them.

The first of these tasks was to return to Raccoon Key to check on the boat. With the storm breaking, I hadn't had time to stow everything away properly. After that, I needed electrical supplies to finish wiring in the dining room. I thought about buying a tarp for the roof, which led me to wonder how I was going to get on the roof to install it. I added the tarp to my list, grabbed my keys, and headed out.

When I arrived at Ethy's house on Raccoon Key, she and Tess were having breakfast in the kitchen. Ethy was in her bathrobe, her hair disheveled. Tess was wearing floral-patterned shorts, a light blue tank top, and sandals, her long brown hair spun into a bun at the back of her head. I'm not immune to the power of feminine

21

eye candy, but with a calendar sitting between them and a lively discussion going on about nails and haircuts, this was not the time to join them. Before I could escape to the dock, Ethy commanded me to sit, but their conversation continued, the subject somehow turning to a poor woman who left a popular nail salon with two bleeding toes and a fungus infection.

To my relief, Detective Murphy appeared, received a warm welcome from Ethy, and was also offered a seat at the table. He politely declined, accepted a cup of coffee, and asked if we could talk a few minutes about the body I'd found.

He followed me to the lanai. "I was headed to Key West on the causeway when I spotted your car," he said, answering a question I had yet to ask. "I figured it was best to talk to you in person."

"That's sounds like what a doctor says before he delivers bad news."

A smile teased the corners of his mouth. "Funny you should say that."

We sat across from each other. Ethy and Tess appeared. Ethy took a seat between the detective and me, folded her arms across her chest, and looked directly at Detective Murphy. "You fellas keep talking. Jake isn't so good with sharing, so if I want to know what's what, I need to hear it firsthand." Tess stood at the doorway.

Detective Murphy opened a folder. "I spent the evening checking missing persons databases, looking for reports of missing children that matched the dead girl's description. I started with the Keys, then expanded the search to the whole state. Keep in mind that not all reports are uploaded and not all missing kids are even reported. Some kids run away, and the parents just don't care. Those are the unwanted ones — in effect, throwaway children."

"Dear God," said Ethy softly.

"It's a hard thing, not being wanted by your mother," said Tess.

The statement drew stares from the three of us. "Sadly," said Detective Murphy, "it happens all too often."

He returned his attention to the folder, flipped through a few pages, then clasped his hands together. "I searched specifically for the butterfly tattoo, but that was just to be thorough. The photo you took didn't provide enough detail to be useful. I submitted a request for a facial reconstruction sketch, but that's going to take time — probably weeks. All this simply confirms what we already knew — that it was going to be difficult to identify her. Again, without knowing who she was, it would be nearly impossible to determine the exact circumstances of her death."

"I heard this last night," I said impatiently. "Nice of you to drop by, but we don't need to rehash the realities."

The detective shook his head. "I get that you're peeved, but honestly you might try listening before you open your yap."

Ethy nodded in agreement, apparently pleased that she and the detective shared an opinion about my general demeanor.

"Even with the photos you took and your observations of the body, the department is going to want more evidence to justify a full investigation. Fantasy Fest Week is about to start and most of the police department's resources are being shifted to deal with the influx of tourists, pickpockets, and drug dealers. We are still waiting on the medical examiner's report, but for now we don't have much to go on."

I nodded. "We wouldn't want the death of a young girl interfering with a holiday dedicated to getting drunk and naked in public."

Detective Murphy closed the file and glared at me. "I've heard about you getting involved in your mother's case. I'm five years from retiring from this shit job, and I'm hoping to get out with my full pension. Generally, that means keeping my head down, doing what I'm told, and not making waves. If that's not clear enough, let me explain it to you. If I have questions, I'll ask you. If you remember something, you'll call me. What you won't do is go poking around in my case. Don't be asking questions or trying to find who she was. All you'll accomplish is alerting potential witnesses and getting in my way. That's the reality, Jake. I suggest you start learning to live with it."

The detective collected his folder and left me with a head full of thoughts. Ethy seemed to be reading them.

"I know you don't care what I think," she said, "but this is a bad idea, even by your standards. If you get involved in this girl's death, it's going to mess you up good. Go fishing or paint a wall or something, but don't do this."

I held up my lists. "Right now, I'm heading to Home Depot. To be fair, sometimes that place messes with my head, but today I think I'm safe. I'll be back this afternoon and take you fishing."

I made no mention of my late mother's emails, in part because I wasn't certain what I was going to do about them, but mostly to spare Ethy a day of fretting about my possible reactions to them.

I took my coffee to the boat and ran the bilge pump to drain the rainwater that had collected in the bottom. After I stowed the anchor in the bow compartment, I confirmed that I had the proper fishing gear for the afternoon's outing. The busy work done, I sat on the dock and tried unsuccessfully to think of something other than Detective Murphy's assessment of the investigation.

The essence of Detective Murphy's reasoning seemed to be without the victim's name, there was nothing to investigate. Of course, without an investigation, her name would most likely remain unknown. Toss in a few complaints about resources and the need to protect his pension, and it was easy to question the detective's commitment to the case.

Detective Murphy had his view of reality, and I had my mine. I probably wasn't going to find out how the dead girl died, but I'd be damned if I'd let her be buried as a Jane Doe.

Before leaving the dock, I called Don Claiborne, a research scientist I'd served with on several lionfish survey outings. The call rolled over to his voicemail. I offered a few social platitudes as a lead-in to asking a favor — scientifically tracking an object carried by currents circulating around southern Florida.

Tess was waiting for me by my car, sipping a diet soda. As I approached, she gazed at me through dark brown eyes, the right corner of her mouth turning upward, creating a small dimple. She was smirking, something she did a lot around me, and something I was beginning to find simultaneously irritating and charming.

"What have I done to amuse you now?" I asked preemptively.

"Not you, or not just you. You know Ethy loves you, right? She picks at you to make certain she doesn't get too close. You call her Ethy and not Mom to keep your distance, but you care about her. It's just funny — and maybe a bit sad — that you two can't acknowledge your feelings after all these years."

"Sounds like you've been in therapy."

"I've had my share of head doctors," agreed Tess. "Did me a lot of good. How about you?"

"Great chat. I'm off to Home Depot, so I'll see you this afternoon."

Tess pursed her lips, then shook her head. "I don't think so."

"Really? You know this how?"

"Because Ethel doesn't think so? Because the detective doesn't think so?" She shrugged. "Maybe because I don't want you to."

"I think I've missed something."

"Ethel is worried that the dead girl you found will remind you of what happened to your mother. I don't know what that means exactly, but from what little she said, I gather your mom was murdered. Anyway, the point is that she doesn't want you to go mental about the dead girl and has assigned me to watch you until it's time to take her fishing. That's because she doesn't believe you're going to Home Depot. I didn't tell Ethel but finding out who the girl was isn't the same as finding out how she died. It really is a whole different thing — something we could do together, because I'm pretty good with people even if you're not."

"I'm good with people," I said defensively.

The smirk returned. "I think I could help."

"Why would you do that?"

"What does it matter? The point is that if you're thinking about talking to girls on the street, you're going to have a tough time. They'll think you're a cop and lie to you. If not a cop, you'll come across as a guy looking for a blow job. They'll ask for your money and then lie to you. That is, if they haven't snatched your wallet. I know a lot of them because I'm an Uber driver on days when I'm not watching your mom. I give some of the girls free rides. Girls talk to girls. They'll talk to me."

When I didn't answer, Tess pushed a cascade of long brown hair off her face. "You don't have much choice because Ethy gave me strict instructions to shadow you. She even gave me money for lunch and instructions on where to buy her a Cuban sandwich. This is a done deal, so tell me where we're going first and let's get on with it."

Being told what to do by Ethy was something I had learned to tolerate. Tess's attitude, which bordered on surly, normally would have provoked a response. But for some inexplicable reason, I found Tess's brashness endearing, almost refreshing.

She climbed into the passenger seat, clicked on her seat belt, and patted the driver's seat with her hand. "You're wasting time."

I started the car and headed out. "First we're going to Home Depot. I need junction boxes. Then we're going to talk to a man who knows everything there is about tattoos."

CHAPTER FOUR

As we headed down Route 1 to Old Town, Tess sat quietly, twirling a lock of hair around her finger. She smiled at me a few times, then pointed out the window. "I think you missed the entrance to Home Depot."

"I don't like being rushed, and I get the feeling you're a dog with a bone. I'll do the Depot later, after I've had time to think about what I need."

"Great! I thought we'd talk to some of the kids who live on the street, see if anyone might have heard anything, unless you're dead set on getting a tattoo first?"

"We could do that, but I'm not sure how much we'd learn when all we have is a vague description of a dead girl. If we dangled a bagel, I'm sure we'd get some bullshit name and address."

"I thought you took photos of the dead girl...."

"I took dozens of photographs, including a few of her face, or what remained of it. Portions of her cheeks and lips were missing, as were her eyes, all most likely eaten by fish and sea scavengers looking for an easy meal. Even her best friend would have to overcome shock and repulsion to look at one of those photos for more than a few seconds. My camera's in the back. You can look at them if you want. I'd rather not."

Tess retrieved the camera, then hesitated. "Maybe later. What's this tattoo guy going to tell us?"

"It happens that I have a slightly out-of-focus shot of the butterfly tattoo on her right thigh." I pulled onto the shoulder of the road, took the camera from her, pressed a few buttons, and handed it back to her. "I don't think the butterfly is a flash tat. I'm hoping it was unique enough that Devin can identify the artist who inked it."

Tess studied the preview screen for a moment. "So, what's a flash tat?"

"A flash tat is a design you pick from a catalogue or off a wall display. They're inexpensive when compared to custom designs, which is what Devin does."

"Who is Devin?"

"An odd man, like a lot of the people who live here. My dad seemed to be one of the few people in Key West he talked to. He took a liking to me after my mother was murdered, even managed to laugh when we played in his swimming pool with his two dogs. The relationship didn't go unnoticed and spawned a rumor that he was my biological father." I shrugged. "He wasn't."

I pulled the car back onto the highway.

Tess put the camera on the back seat, then wedged herself against the car door so she could face me. "Ethy said your mother was murdered when you were four and that you were the one who found her. That's a hard way to start childhood."

"Ethy talks too much."

"So, it's true?"

30

"Let me say this once, not because I'm upset or being defensive, but so you understand why this isn't something I want to talk about. When the police arrived at our house, I was sitting beside my mother. I was covered with blood and holding a gun. The gun was..."

Tess touched my shoulder. "Sorry. Sorry. I shouldn't have pried. I ask a lot of questions... Shit. That must have been awful."

"I'm a bit prickly sometimes and get moody when the subject comes up, so it's probably best that you hear the story from me and then let it go. What I was going to say is that the gun was an automatic that had a grip safety, so it was virtually impossible for a four-year-old with a small hand to fire it. That didn't stop people from speculating that I was the shooter. When I started school, I was taunted by kids calling my mother a whore and saying I killed her. They got that shit from their parents, but that's what I contended with most of my early life. In time, I grew bigger than most kids my age and took the opportunity to kick the shit out of a few of them, but that led to other problems.

"When I was about fourteen, I started demanding that the police reopen her case. Ethy thinks I went mental, but Maurice understood I was just frustrated. I'm going to spare you the details but think of it as a delayed case of PTSD. Maurice arranged for me to work on a boat looking for shipwrecks that summer. The captain was a patient man — anyone looking for treasure has to be. Three months on the water and we found nothing, which helped me accept the likelihood that some mysteries never get solved. Of course, it's more complicated than that, but that's the gist of it."

Tess's shook her head. "I can't imagine...Damn. All that comes to mind is an assortment of clichés and a hundred questions about working as a treasure hunter, which I'll save for later.

31

Anyway, now that I know why you're so fucked up, I think I like you better."

"Well, I'm glad you understood the essence of the story, which could have been easily missed. Anyway, Ethy frets about me because of what happened in high school. She's telling you things because she's worried I'm going to be obsessed with the dead girl I found. Personally, I think there are better things to talk about than my weird childhood, like lionfish and invasive species and what to wear for the Fantasy Fest Parade."

I drove slowly down Duval Street. A few blocks from Devin's studio, Tess pointed at a car pulling out of a space. I stopped behind the car while another car stopped in front of it. She jumped out and directed other cars around me. Serenaded by a cacophony of honking horns and angry voices, I pulled into the space, unsure whether it was legitimately mine but pleased with the small victory nonetheless.

The street was swarming with tourists, some shopping for costumes and masks, a few already in festival dress. We passed several commercial stores offering flash tattoos, T-shirts, and sex toys.

Tess stood in the doorway of one of the large shops and stared at a wall full of designs, images, and slogans. "I always wonder why a woman would permanently inscribe the name of some guy on her ass or her boob without knowing whether the guy would turn out to be a loser. I mean, I've got enough trouble forgetting mistakes I made. I don't need to be reminded of them every time I take a shower or bath; and what do you say to your next boyfriend? 'Oh, don't worry, Buzz is my brother?'" Tess looked at me. "Sorry. That was weird."

"No more than usual. To be fair, I've often thought the same thing, although to be honest, Buzz and I weren't that close."

A woman walked towards us dressed like a gangster, or so it appeared. Tess stared at her, then turned as she passed by. "That woman wasn't wearing clothes," she said. "I mean, her costume was painted on."

"Body paint is a popular option with some festival goers. A cop will probably tell her it's a bit early to be minimally attired, but later in the week, no one will care." Tess continued to stare as other tourists took pictures. "The festival lasts ten days, features dozens of parties, marches, street fairs, and concerts. The whole thing ends this Saturday with the Fantasy Fest parade and party night. I believe the theme this year is Prohibition, which explains why she's wearing a zoot suit."

"But she isn't."

I pulled Tess away and we continued down Duval Street.

In order to find Devin's studio, you had to know the address. Other than the street number and the words "BY APPOINTMENT ONLY," the entrance to his studio was unmarked.

Tess reached to open the door, but I stopped her. "Devin's always been nice to me, but to most folks he displays all the personality of a feral cat. Maurice once told me that Devin went to prison as a young man for stealing food. He drew the attention of some of the older inmates and was quickly the prized toy of his cell block. I was too young to grasp the full meaning of what Maurice was saying but understood instinctively that Devin had been mistreated. Anyway, Devin learned to be a scratcher in prison, inking tattoos with nothing more than a needle and whatever dye he could scrounge from prison supplies. He was incredibly talented. His art made him a prison superstar, and that status stopped the rapes. When Devin was released, Maurice loaned him the money to buy professional equipment and got him an apprenticeship with

33

an ink man in Miami. He does custom work at custom prices but, from looking at him, you would never know that he's a rich man."

"What's your point?"

"You need to understand that he may not be happy to see us. If he gets worked up, don't personalize it."

"I can't wait to meet him."

I pushed opened the door and was greeted by the jingling of bells. A moment later, a loud voice came from behind a counter. "Can't you fucking read?"

When I didn't answer, Devin's face appeared above the counter, his dark eyes glaring at the illiterate intruders who had invaded his space. "Hey, Dev," I said cheerfully.

A moment passed before his expression softened. "God damn it, Jake. I was a second away from shooting you. Maybe I should anyway."

I introduced Tess and handed Devin my cellphone so he could see my photo of the butterfly tattoo. "Any idea who might have inked this?"

"No," he said, throwing the phone back to me.

"The tat is on a dead girl I found yesterday floating in the Gulf. This butterfly is all I have to figure out who she is. I'd be appreciative if you'd look again."

Devin took the phone and this time studied it carefully. "It's not art you get from a tourist shop. I'm almost certain it's a custom job, but not a local one. I'm guessing that's a young girl's ass holding up the ink. Most kids don't have the money for this kind of work. I think there's a small geometric in the thorax and something else in the wing, but the picture isn't clear enough for me to say for sure. Get me a better photo and I might be able to determine if the artist left a signature."

I thanked him and was about to leave when he handed me a flyer. "I found this stuck to my door this morning. You're looking for a dead girl and someone's looking for a live one." The flyer included an image of a teenaged girl who, though smiling, projected an innate sadness. According to the flyer, the girl, Alicia, had emotional issues that required medication. Anyone seeing her was asked to call a number but not approach her. An unspecified reward was offered for information leading to her return.

"Doesn't say who's looking for her," I said.

Devin shook his head. "I'd bet my gold fillings it ain't her parents. Thing is, I know her. Once and a while I see her singing with the ladies at the Open Arms Congregation off Jasper Street. She didn't seem to have emotional issues to me. What she had was too much make-up and clothes a hooker might wear. She had a friend, a younger girl dressed and made-up the same way. I don't know if her friend is your dead chick, but I'm just saying you might want to find Alicia and ask her."

He told me I could keep the flyer and disappeared behind the counter.

When we stepped back onto Duval Street, Tess snatched the flyer from my hand. "You know some interesting people."

She studied the flyer for a moment. "We probably pass a dozen girls like Alicia every time we walk down Duval Street, but we never look them in the face. They're invisible people with miserable pasts and no futures." She glanced at me. "Now all the kids will be looking, hoping to get the reward. They won't talk to us about Alicia or the girl you found. At least not for free."

"I've got work to do," I said.

Tess gave me a steely glance, then turned her attention back to the flyer. "You know as well as I do that the police will never look for this girl, even if she knows something about the dead girl. They don't have the time, the resources, or any reason to. Devin said something about a church. We could take a few minutes to see if anyone there has seen Alicia. I mean, someone has to."

What Tess was proposing was not an original thought. Besides visiting the church, I was already considering how I might get Devin a better picture of the tattoo. I also was trying to work out how I might track down a sailor named Steven. In my way of thinking, these three separate tasks were best done alone. But I was resigned to having Tess shadow me until it was time to take Ethy fishing. There was nothing to gain by delaying until I was free of her.

"Alright. Let's visit the Open Arms church and see if anyone's seen her."

"Maybe you can show me your house on the way to the church," Tess said. When I didn't respond, she added, "I need to pee."

*****

I drove to my house and parked in the driveway. The biological imperative was quickly addressed, but Tess insisted on a tour. I cautioned her not to touch anything because the walls hadn't been painted and the drywall compound was still shedding. I also warned her to watch her feet around the stacks of debris and the maze of extension cords.

In the living room, where bare electrical wires protruded from the walls and ceiling, she puffed out her cheeks and emitted a soft groan. "You live here?"

"It's not so bad."

36

"It's tiny. I mean, a card table would about fill the room. I can't imagine raising a family in such a small space."

"You have to remember that for a lot of folks, living in Key West is about having a place just to sleep and to eat a meal. Most of my time growing up here was spent on boats or snorkeling or diving. Family gatherings happened in the street. So, yeah, it's small but it's functional."

She scanned the room, then looked at the floor near the front door. "Is this where you found your mother?" She quickly turned to me. "I'm so sorry. I...I did it again. Things just pop into my head. I don't mean to be cruel."

I cleared my throat and took a slow breath. "Here's what I think I remember. I had a bad dream and went to get into her bed, but I couldn't find her. When I came in here, I saw her lying on the floor. Her eyes were open, so I knew she wasn't sleeping. Even at four, I knew she was dead." I walked to the spot and kneeled down. "I think I can still see a dark stain in the wood, but no one else can. I mean, it's been over twenty years."

I took another deep breath, willing away a moment of sadness.

"Sorry," I said as I stood up. "Sometimes..."

Tess nodded. "I barely knew my mother," she said. "My dad was an electronics wizard for the army. They were always sending him some place that needed protection from surveillance. After we moved for the tenth time, my mother left for good. I was young and don't remember any discussion of me going with her. My assumption was that she didn't want me. Maybe that's why I have no real memories of her. Yeah, it hurts even now, so I get it. Anyway, I'm sorry that I keep bringing it up...Maybe we should go."

"Is your dad retired?"

"No," she said, shaking her head. "He's dead. Really smart man, but he didn't have a degree and wasn't an officer. The chain of command is full of people who know nothing and won't listen. An incident on base required someone to take the blame. Shit rolls downhill. He was given a dishonorable discharge and went home to drink himself to death." She glanced at the floor, then at me. "I guess we're both orphans in a manner of speaking."

"Good to get it all out there," I said.

Tess laughed. "I know this is going to surprise you, but some people are actually more fucked up than we are. I don't know any, but I'm sure they're out there somewhere."

There were, and we were about to meet them.

CHAPTER FIVE

The sun flirted with clouds billowing in the western sky. A soft southern breeze carried fragrances of cuisines as varied as the peoples who had settled here. On city street corners, folks eager for company collected, their laughter a momentary escape from the hard realities of surviving on an island at the end of the road.

As we navigated our way to the church where Alicia sang, Tess peppered me with questions. Some I chose to answer, others I deflected.

"You grew up in a bar?"

I stepped around a utility pole that seemed to grow from the center of the sidewalk then waited for Tess to catch up.

"I grew up like a lot of kids around here with parents who worked when others didn't. When I came home from school, I went to the bar because that's where they were. Some of the musicians would hang out there and jam. Doing math to the sound of a minor key riff played by a sax and countered by a trumpet was normal. My teacher in high school attributed my math skills to that music. The only regret I have is that I never acquired the skill to play what I heard in my head. I wrote a couple of tunes that were adapted by a really good keyboard player. By *adapted*, I mean that when he was done with them, you'd never recognize the tune I wrote, but he gave me credit anyway. That was cool. When I was ten, Maurice taught me to how to drive a boat, and how to mix an Old-Fashioned. Hard to complain about growing up here."

"Maurice sounds like a nice man."

A tour train passed us, its speaker blaring factoids at tired and sunburned tourists.

"His real kids didn't seem to share his enthusiasm for the water, treasure hunting, jazz, blues, diving. Then I came along. We enjoyed all of it, together, until I got older and he got older. The business changed and money became tight. Over time, the music of Key West wasn't enough to compete with the titty bars, or cafés that catered to coffee snobs. Ethy and Maurice had to decide whether to go dirty or sell the bar."

"What happened?"

"The year I graduated from high school, Maurice accepted a developer's offer to buy the bar. The money was good, and it was the smart thing to do, but Ethy cried for a month. I think I did as well. But then Maurice surprised us with a new house on Raccoon Key. Ethy wasn't keen on living in New Town, but once she got used to not working, having a boat dock, and living normal hours, she came around. I went off to college on a scholarship. Kind of the American dream. Two years later, Maurice died. She still hasn't forgiven him for leaving her and takes it out on me. Most of the time, I let it roll off me, but other times…"

I finished the thought with a shrug. To my relief, Tess didn't press me further. A few minutes later, the sound of voices wafted toward us as we took in the church's faded white steeple rising above the palm trees. We were treated to a gospel sung loud and enthusiastically to a counter melody that bordered on jazz played on an organ. Listeners outside the church clapped and sang and rocked. If God was in the vicinity, I'm certain He or She was tapping a foot.

When the song ended, the church began to empty. We waited until the door was clear and stepped inside. Coming towards us was a black man with the build of a linebacker wearing a Bob Marley T-shirt and dark glasses.

"I'm sorry, but we aren't open for visitors," he said, smiling broadly. "We will be starting a board meeting in about five minutes but would love for you to join us on another evening or Sunday. I don't ask for anything, but of course donations fuel the Lord's work."

"Actually, we're looking for someone." I showed him the flyer of Alicia. He looked at it for a moment, then handed it back. "You related to this girl?"

The question struck me as odd. That his answer might depend on how I was connected to Alicia suggested he knew something he wasn't willing to volunteer.

Before I could answer, he said: "No, I haven't seen her," his words clipped and tinged with anger. "Lots of street trash hangs out here when the choir sings. Some just listen, others steal. Now, if you will excuse me…"

"A young girl is dead and the girl on this flyer may have known her," I said. "Maybe someone here saw them together. One of them liked to sing. Would you mind if we asked around?"

"I would mind. Couple of white girls get in a bind, and the two of you come here for help. When black and brown girls go missing, no one thinks twice about them. I don't wish those girls any harm, but what happens to them isn't my problem."

The harsh words from a supposed man of the cloth stunned me. "I'm sorry. I guess it isn't. We didn't mean to intrude."

Tess stopped at the front of the church. "What crawled up him?"

I heard a woman's voice behind me. "That poor child."

We turned and saw a large, round-faced woman sporting a dirty pair of reading glasses hanging from a chain around her neck. "Don't let Preacher Simmons frighten you," she said in a soft voice. "He carries a heavy burden and sometimes says things he doesn't mean. But I never heard him bust on white people like that. Something powerful must be troubling him for him to say what he did. I'll give him a good talking-to."

She walked toward us with a slight limp. "I can't walk too good in these shoes on account of a bunion I have on my left foot. Damnedest thing. For sixty years, I could walk anywhere. Then one day, I felt this little tiny bump. The next day, is was like a walnut growing on the side of my big toe. It's a good thing our Fantasy Fest concert don't require any walking, or I'd be hollering more than singing."

She beamed at me, then touched my cheek. "My name is Clara — Clara Morse. Just like the Code. I don't know the code, but I say that 'cause it makes it easy for folks to remember. You might not remember me 'cause the last time you saw me you were only six or so. I used to take care of you before and after your momma died."

I stared at her, finding something familiar in her bright eyes and caring smile. Then it dawned on me. "Oh my God, I do remember," I said, wrapping my arms around her. "You made shrimp and grits, right? And a creole with okra."

"Not many little kids liked adult food, but you would try anything. My, my." She pressed her palms into my shoulders and

42

examined me. "Now you're all grown up and married to a beautiful girl."

"This is Tess Simpson…"

"We're not married," said Tess.

"Give it time. He'll come to his senses. So, what brings you to this part of town?"

I handed Clara the flyer. "Did you know this girl?"

Clara slipped on her reading glasses. "Your daddy used to come by my house after my husband died and helped fix things. I came to his funeral. Such a nice man. Yes. Yes. I first saw this girl a few times last year. She loved the music. You know, I heard her singing along a few times. She had voice that needed a bit of training, but my god it was sweet to hear. Wore a lot of makeup, that child did. You kind of know she's doing the streets. The last time I saw her was maybe a week ago. Pretty sure it was her. It was the evening, not quite dark. She tried to get into the church, but it was locked up. I didn't see where she went after that, but my guess is Miss Rachael's. The next day, some man comes by asking about her. A day after that, kids are handing out these flyers. Trouble was following her that night, and it's looking for her now. That's the truth."

She gave us directions to Miss Rachael's, then patted my hand. "You grew up real good. I know you had your troubles, but I always knew you were special. You come by our concert, hear?"

I hugged her again. Then she wrapped her arms around Tess. "If he don't do you right, you come to me and I'll beat some sense into him." She laughed. "Lord knows I will. All men need a good whooping to get them seeing straight. Jake here is probably overdue."

As we walked away, Tess smiled. "Can I adopt her as my mother? Is that legal?"

Rachael's house was a small two-story Victorian structure with a wraparound porch on the lower level and a smaller veranda off the second story. As we approached, three girls of varying ages scurried inside. Before we reached the first step to the porch, we were confronted by a heavyset woman who looked to be in her fifties and was holding a broom. I wasn't certain what purpose the broom served, but it added to her don't-mess-with-me look.

Tess and I offered friendly platitudes, which were rewarded with a cold stare and an indifferent tone. "Is there something you want?"

I held up the flyer. "A young girl was found dead yesterday. We'd like to speak to Alicia to see if she can tell us the dead girl's name."

Rachael stared at us, calculating a response. "I'm sorry to hear about the girl who died, but I can't tell you anything about Alicia. You may be telling the truth, or you're just some folks one of these kids is running away from. I'm not inclined to find out it's the latter." She turned and went inside.

Tess stared at the empty porch. "Well, so far we've met a man of God with a lot of attitude, a church lady who knew you as a baby and still cares about you, and a woman who protects runaways like a momma bear. Lots of local charm but can't say we learned much."

"I thought the preacher went out of his way to keep us from looking around or coming back. My take is he was being rude on purpose. Rachael said she wouldn't tell us about Alicia, not that she didn't know anything about her."

"You think she's been here?"

"I do. She might still be here or at the church. These folks aren't going to tell us anything until they trust us, which could be never. We need to figure out a different approach before we come back."

On the walk back to the car, Tess talked alternately about lunch and Alicia.

"The flyer says she's got emotional issues and needs medication. As Devin remembered her, she was caked with makeup and dressed like a hooker. Going with Devin, it sounds to me like she's hiding from her pimp. If that's true, then maybe the dead girl you found was also doing tricks and pissed off the same guy."

"Which would explain why the preacher and Rachael are so keen on protecting Alicia."

Tess stepped in front of me and stopped. "We need to get a better picture of the butterfly tattoo and see if Devin can identify who inked it," she said, waving the flyer at me. "Alicia is in trouble. Someone has got to help her."

"Remember," I said, "this is a police matter. We're only gathering data and giving it to Detective Murphy."

A furrow deepened across Tess' forehead and she stared into my eyes. "You don't believe that. I know you don't." Her voice rose as her face reddened. "The cops didn't care about your mother and they don't care now. That's what you're thinking."

I walked past her without answering.

"We have to do something."

I turned and faced her. "*We* don't have do anything, and *you* don't know what I'm thinking. Hell, I don't know what I'm thinking. I know you mean well, but you've taken a few facts you've learned about my past and cobbled together a profile of me — that's fucked up. I'm not angry with you. I like you, but when you do that, it's beyond irritating."

45

I reminded her of my promise to Ethy of lunch and then an afternoon of fishing. Tess stayed in the car at the café, declining my offer of a sandwich or a drink. On the drive back to Raccoon Key, she sat quietly, playing with a strand of hair and avoided looking at me.

As a peace offering, I told her the story of how Maurice acquired the boat without Ethy knowing about it. Ethy complained afterward, but always insisted on a weekly fishing trip to one of the many small keys nearby. "Before each trip, she'd say, 'If you're dumb enough to have a boat, you might as well enjoy it.' She hasn't said that lately, but if she's still mad at me about yesterday, you might get an earful today."

"Okay. Thanks for sharing."

"If you'd rather stay..."

"No. I'm going on the boat. Just... don't like being barked at. I'm not saying I didn't deserve it. Just give me a few minutes to decide if I should tell Ethel you were mean to me."

Having two females pissed off at me at the same time was a new experience. Tess was angry because I hadn't done enough to help Alicia. Ethy preferred that I work on my house and leave the investigation of Jane Doe to Detective Murphy. I decided to let them sort out their grievances against me on their own. We left the dock with Tess still in a snit and Ethy unaware that Tess and I weren't speaking.

Things seemed to thaw when Ethy demanded to see the place where I'd found the body. Tess thought it was a great idea despite my insistence there was nothing to see but water in all directions — that there were better places to fish. My objections were to no avail. Ethy reminded me the boat was hers, and she could decide where it went.

The two of them asked questions about the body, about what it was doing way out here, how it got here. When I offered a tutorial on floating objects in current fields, the questions turned to Alicia and why someone was looking for her. When this speculation didn't prove interesting, Ethy asked if I was looking for Alicia. I explained that it was possible Alicia knew the dead girl, and so I'd made a few inquiries about Alicia and her whereabouts. Tess stirred the pot, saying we hadn't seen any sign the police were trying to find out who the dead girl was or where Alicia might be. My rejoinder that undercover police activity is not meant to be seen didn't prevent Ethy from lamenting how sad it was that no one was trying to help a helpless girl. This prompted another heartfelt tirade from Tess that no child should be left unprotected.

I anchored the boat in a sandy area near the reef where I'd first encountered the body of the young woman. While Tess and Ethy engaged in a circular discussion about helping children in trouble and not getting involved, I put on my gear and rolled into the water with my camera and short spear. The sound of my heartbeat and the air escaping my regulator quickly replaced the chatter of human voices. Surrounded by water, the noise in my head subsided. Moments later, I was looking for lionfish in the shallow reef.

I was quickly rewarded. The population of lionfish I'd seen the other day was still lurking about the coral heads, as beautiful as they were dangerous. Without any natural predators, a lionfish is fearless, allowing me, with my camera and later my spear, to approach within inches. I took photos and made a mental count of the fish that swam by me in a ten-minute interval. Before surfacing, I speared a dozen unsuspecting fish and loaded them into a puncture-proof fish containment unit specially designed to keep the venomous spines from poking through.

When I came up and back onto the boat, I handed Tess the container of fish, and she held up my phone. "A guy looking for a deck hand called. I didn't get his name, but he said he heard about you from some other guy I can't remember. A guy named Don Claiborne, who seemed nice but wanted to know more about a current study you asked for. Detective Murphy. Not really sure why, but it sounded like he wanted to make nice. He did say something about caviar and a meeting at the medical examiner's office tomorrow morning at 8:30. You should call him. Are these lionfish?"

"They are. What's this about a meeting?"

"Are we going to fish or just jabber?" snapped Ethy.

"Are they poisonous?" asked Tess.

"Venomous. The top and lower spines can sting you but cooking them destroys the venom. The container can't be punctured, so you're safe."

"Can we go now?" demanded Ethy.

I pulled up the anchor and drove the boat close to a small key. While I called Detective Murphy, Ethy sat in a chair next to Tess at the stern and tossed a lure toward the shore.

"What's this about caviar?" I said.

"Kids go out on party boats to drink, use drugs, whatever. They eat chips and burgers. This kid had been eating caviar. I don't like the stuff, but even if I did, I can't afford it. You mentioned a pricey tattoo and expensive makeup. Now we have expensive food. Got me to thinking that I may have come across as…"

"An asshole."

"Wasn't the first thing that came to mind, but okay."

"Is there something else?"

"Let's say that I'm warming to the idea that the victim's death wasn't accidental. Maybe with a better photograph of her tattoo, I could find out where she got it."

"You won't find her tat on-line. I know some people but none who would talk to a cop."

Detective Murphy groaned softly. "You do realize I'm asking you to help me?"

"What about making waves and your pension?"

This time I heard a long slow sigh. "Sometimes, shit happens to change your perspective. If I'm going to solve this case, I have to hurry. That said, I know someone in the ME's office. I can get you in and out faster and with less hassle than a police photographer."

"When?"

"Tomorrow. Eight-thirty."

"Tomorrow then."

I joined Ethy and Tess at the back of the boat. Tess turned and smiled at me; her face lit up by the soft orange rays of the setting sun. A feeling of relief flickered through my head that perhaps she'd forgiven me for snapping at her. I was about to ask when I saw Ethy's pole bend sharply toward the water. "Get the net!" she shrieked. "Get the goddamned net!"

That evening, we dined on blackened grouper, lionfish, and sautéed bok choy. I told Tess about my meeting with Detective Murphy, after which she announced she had to leave and would meet me at the medical examiner's office in the morning. I started to object, but she smirked and shook her head.

Shortly after dinner, Ethy dozed off for the third time. I woke her and suggested she should get ready for bed. I promised I would clean the kitchen so that it wouldn't smell like fish in the morning.

After a lecture about cleaning the sink with lemon juice and a reminder of how my dad promised to do the same and didn't, she headed to her room.

With the house smelling of lemon, I loaded the trash into a bin at the side of the house and headed back to Key West. Halfway down the causeway, I received a call from Don.

"Tracking objects carried in ocean currents is a complicated business. Of course, that you're asking about it raises a whole bunch of questions, starting with what the fuck are you up to and why did you turn down the job you always wanted?"

"About ten miles east of Marathon Key, I found a body floating face down. I want to know where it entered the water and who put it there."

"I'm guessing you don't trust the cops to figure that out."

"Let's just say they don't seem to be in a hurry to spend money investigating the death of a teenaged girl, much less a runaway with no connections to this community."

"Here's the thing: I can run a crude simulation that might give you a rough idea of the entry point, but it could be off by miles. What you need is software that incorporates models of the oceanic state, the atmospheric state — basically wind magnitude and direction, the surface wave field in the region of interest. That data is not only hard to come by but requires a powerful computer to crunch the numbers. I know a guy who might have access to the software and data. Because it's not quite legal, it'll be expensive."

"Send me his phone number and —"

"This guy wears a tin foil hat and has had his fillings removed. He isn't just *whoo-whoo* paranoid; he believes insects are actually bots that are listening to his thoughts. I know him because we're in the business of tracking and salvaging flotsam and jetsam."

"You dumpster-dive the ocean?"

"He won't talk to you. If he agrees to help you, you'll need to supply me a good estimate of when the body was thrown in the water. We're assuming that the body didn't sink, that it floated from the time it went into the water until you found it. If there's water in the lungs, it most likely sank and only surfaced after decomposition gases made it buoyant. If that's the case, the model results probably won't be very meaningful."

I told Don about my upcoming meeting at the ME's office and agreed to get him the information he requested.

"You're sure you want to do this, Jake? Chasing down this girl's death is admirable, but it sounds like something that could mess you up again."

I assured him I wouldn't let that happen. I wasn't sure he believed me.

*****

Detective Murphy called just after midnight. "I thought you'd be the pain in the ass, not your girlfriend."

I heard the voice through a beer fog and grappled to understand what I was being told.

"You're calling about Tess? What…"

She was picked up in a residential area after a call came in from a community watch volunteer. Apparently, she was outside a house used to shelter runaways, watching the front door. She pretended to be on the phone, but the arresting officer checked on her anyway. He also said she seemed uncooperative, whatever that means, and resisted arrest. I told you I'd toss you under the bus if I had to, but I convinced the officer to give your girlfriend a pass.

51

If anyone asks, you two got into a pissing contest, and she left in a huff. She's at the station waiting for a ride home."

Fifteen minutes later, I walked into the station. Tess stood up and walked past me.

"Still pissed," said the desk sergeant. "I don't envy your night with her."

I slid into the driver's seat and clicked my seatbelt. "You don't want to talk about this, do you?"

"You can be perceptive."

"Should I drive you to your car or to Ethy's?"

Tess pressed her head against the window glass. "I couldn't get the image of Alicia's face out of my mind. I…fuck. Not everything is about you." She turned and grabbed my hand. "I didn't mean it like that. I'm…Fuck! I shouldn't talk. I just make it worse."

"Tell me."

She pressed her head into her hands. "Where to start?"

"Beginnings are good."

"Here's the thing: Ethy thinks this case is going to set you off because of what happened with your mom. But I'm the one going bonkers. When I was about thirteen, my dad was on assignment in India, doing consulting work for India's defense department. Anyway, we were living in a nice residential area. I met a local girl. She might have been a year older than me. No more. She spoke English and taught me Hindi mixed with a bit of Bengali. Together, we roamed the village and talked and … it was so natural. Then one day, I went to her house and was told she didn't live there anymore."

"Was she sent off to school?"

"Hell no. She was married off to some fat guy with a lot of money! I mean, who the fuck gets married at fourteen? How do you arrange the rest of your child's life? I was so angry that the police came. I was accused of cursing, which might be true, and threatening to attack my friend's mother with a brick. Again, the whole thing was overblown. I embarrassed my father because the man my friend married was well connected. Even our embassy had to step in to make things better. I was locked in our house until my dad's assignment was completed, but I didn't care because I didn't want to go out. I hated that place and the culture that treated women — girls — like property. Something about the girl you found, that dickhead detective's attitude, and Alicia being hunted by a pimp just set me off."

"What did you hope to accomplish?"

Tess shrugged. "I don't know. I…just wanted to talk to her. It was stupid. Can we leave?"

I started the car. "You said you thought some people were more fucked up than we are. I'm not so sure."

Tess laughed. "Probably not."

DAY 3

TUESDAY, OCTOBER 20

CHAPTER SIX

The Monroe County Medical Examiner's Office is housed in a sand-colored, single story structure on Grassy Key in Marathon. In Florida, it is the medical examiner's job to determine what caused a person to die. I was eager to hear what the ME had concluded.

As I entered the lobby, Detective Murphy and Tess were conversing with a middle-aged woman wearing a white coat. A badge identified her as Vicky Wolfe, Director of Operations. After I introduced myself, she stepped back, addressing us as a group.

"Detective Murphy has brought you here to identify the body, which we all know is bullshit because of the condition of her face. That said, I'm going to take you to a room where you can view the body. It's covered with a sheet and will not be uncovered unless the detective specifically asks me to do so. Keep in mind that our Jane Doe was in the water for at least several days, during which her face and hands were subject to predatory fish and crustaceans. Some people find it hard to view a human body degraded in that way. Please don't pass out or vomit. Just leave the room. Now, follow me, please."

When Vicky was a few steps ahead, Detective Murphy turned to me, his jaw clenched. "After we spoke, I got a call from my

CO wanting to know why I'd intervened in the arrest of a woman acting suspiciously in a residential neighborhood. I made up a bullshit story, but this is exactly the crap I wanted to avoid. You take your pictures and that's it. Ask a few more questions if you have to, then go back to whatever miserable life you had before this dead girl showed up."

Inside the room, the cold air was thick with the smell of disinfectant. A sheet-covered gurney was situated in the center of the room. Vicky looked at Tess and me and folded her hands across her waist. "If the detective asks to see the body, you may want to leave the room or at least turn your head. We don't do any reconstructive work here. Some seasoned professionals get overwhelmed by what they see, so you shouldn't feel embarrassed if you need to turn away. What we don't want is for someone to faint and potentially hurt themselves."

"How did she die?" asked Detective Murphy. When Vickie hesitated, the detective shook his head. "Just tell us. I mean, she's a Jane Doe for God's sake. It's not like you're violating her privacy."

Vicky glared at him, then opened a folder. "The victim suffered a serious injury to the spinal cord in her neck, causing instant paralysis and death. We refer to that as the cause of death. How the injury came about is the manner of death. The injury appears to have been induced by the thrusting of her head backwards, as might have occurred had she been grabbed from behind. She also had high levels of Valium and alcohol in her system and could have simply fallen awkwardly, although there is no bruising, and no contusion on her forehead. While the injuries are consistent with death by homicide, they also could be explained as the result of a boating accident. While we know the cause of death, the manner of death isn't definitively known. We may do additional studies to determine whether the manner of death can be determined conclusively."

"Time of death?" asked Detective Murphy.

"Hard to say exactly, but sometime between two and three days ago."

Detective Murphy scribbled something in his notebook. "Was she raped?"

"She had been sexually active, but any direct evidence of being sexually assaulted was compromised by her immersion in salt water."

"She was just a baby," said Tess, her voice quivering. "Who does this to a child?"

Vicky shook her head. "I don't know."

"How about water in the lungs?" I asked.

Vicky flipped through the report. "She didn't drown, if that's what you're asking. Also, because you found her floating face down, there would be no way for the air inside the lungs to escape and water to intrude. So, no, she was already dead when she entered the water."

"Was the caviar in her stomach fully digested?" I asked.

Detective Murphy took the report from Vicky's hand, then glanced at me. "What's your point?" he said.

"Caviar is generally served at lunch or dinner," I replied. "She died almost immediately after she ate. That means she went into the water sometime between noon and nine on one of those two days."

"How's that's helpful?" Murphy asked.

The answer was that it was data I needed to give Don. I shrugged. "Just thinking out loud."

The detective handed the report back to Vicky, then turned to me. "Take your photos and let's get out of here."

Inadvertently, in orienting the corpse to provide a clear shot of the tattoo, the sheet slid off her face, sending Tess for the door. Even Detective Murphy turned away.

I finished shooting the tattoo and was about to leave when Vicky stopped me. "It's not my place to question a report, particularly in front of the detective in charge, but this girl had been repeatedly assaulted by older, large men." Vicky clenched her jaw, her anger obvious, even as she whispered. "I have seen a lot of what people do to each other. Sometimes it takes a bit of time to forget it and move on. But she was just a child, Mr. Savage. The men who did this to her are out there, still alive and probably pretty pleased with themselves. What they did to this girl will stick with me for a long time. I'm not the ME, but my gut tells me this girl was murdered. She was most likely penetrated from behind by a powerful man who grabbed her head and snapped her neck. That's not a scientific conclusion, but I'd put money on it. I don't know who you are or why you're involved, but I hope you can do something to make sure the guy who did this is caught and punished."

I told Vicky I'd do what I could. She pulled the sheet over the body, then held the door open, signaling it was time for me to leave. When I arrived in the lobby, both Tess and Detective Murphy were exiting restrooms.

I looked at Tess. "You okay?"

"No. I'm not sure how you can be."

Detective Murphy shook his head. "It's been a while since I saw something like that. I've seen gang hits, guys beaten to death with bats, and faces blown away with shotguns, but a teenage girl…" He looked at me. "You still think she was murdered?"

I nodded. "The odds of her falling face-down in the water are pretty small. The bruising on her shoulders, the spinal cord injury,

58

the caviar in her stomach…too many facts don't fit the accident scenario."

"You take the tattoo photo and ask around, but don't do anything stupid. Tell me what you learn, and if it's useful, I'll take it from there. Clear?"

I said it was and Detective Murphy lumbered away, his shoulders bent and his head down.

"I'm not sure he could win a game of *Clue*," said Tess.

After walking out, we found Detective Murphy leaning against the side of his car. A moment later, he slid behind the wheel and drove off.

"Did Detective Murphy seem ill to you?" I said. "He was sweating when he came in, and he leaned against the wall a few times."

Tess shrugged. "Didn't notice and don't really care. He just rubs me the wrong way. Anyway, I've got to take your mother to her doctor's appointment today. Afterward, she promised me lunch and a trip to the hair salon. She says my hair is too long for this climate and wants me to get it cut short. She also asked me if you and I were dating."

"Okay, I'll do 'Dating for a hundred.'"

"Well, of course I told her we weren't. Jesus."

"What's the hair thing?"

"I'm thinking about it. I was once a blonde. I might decide to be one again." Tess shrugged. "Sounds trivial compared to what we just saw."

"As we both know, life goes on."

I turned and headed to my car.

"Wait. I need to say this. You've been really patient with all my questions, and I've given you attitude in return. I told you I left behind a bit of baggage in New York.

I'm still dealing with it. It's complicated. Are we okay?"

"I'll see you later," I said.

*****

The drive from Marathon to Key West normally takes about an hour, which would allow me time to plan and re-plan the rest of my day. My priority was to show the photos of the butterfly tattoo to Devin. He wouldn't be in his studio until closer to eleven, which gave me an hour to kill. I had time to make a run at Home Depot. But once again, I drove past the orange entrance sign, this time turning left on First Street and navigating to the parking lot of Key West High School.

For a minute or so, I gazed at the school, waiting to feel a tinge of nostalgia, but it never came. I didn't hate my four years there, but neither could I separate the darker times of my teenage years from things that happened there.

I walked to the office, where I was greeted by a male student fighting a losing battle with acne. I explained that I was looking for yearbooks that might go back thirty years or so, that I hadn't found them online and would like permission to visit the library. The student handed me a clipboard and a short pencil. "Fill this in," he said in a monotone.

Before I could start, a small woman with a beautiful crop of white hair appeared at the desk. "That won't be necessary," she said in a warbling voice. "You're Jake Savage. I taught you Math your senior year. You might not remember —"

"Mrs. Donaldson! How are you?"

"I was very proud to read your paper in *Marine Science Magazine* about the statistical modeling of fish populations." She emitted a squeaky laugh. "I only understood about half of it, but it's always satisfying to see one of your kids accomplishing great things. What can I help you with?"

"I'm doing a bit of research for a friend who's writing a book. I won't bore you with the details, but he wants to know if any alumni of this school went into the navy. I can't imagine why, but there's no explaining what people write books about."

"How far back are you talking?"

"Thirty years or so."

"We don't always know where kids go after graduation. I'm afraid the yearbooks won't help much. Look at the comments page. If someone enlisted before graduation, it might be noted on the 'Seniors of Note' page." She handed me a slip of paper. "Show this to the police officer in the hall. I hope you find what you're really looking for."

I didn't. I searched back thirty-two years, to five years before I was born. Almost a dozen guys named James graduated from Key West High School during that time. None of them did anything to earn a spot on the 'Seniors of Note' page, meaning my dad was a nobody or he wasn't local.

I left the school with a bad feeling. Some things never change.

*****

I drove to my house, transferred the photographs of Jane Doe's thigh to my iPad, and walked back to Devin's studio in Old Town. He groused again about my not having an appointment and being interrupted, then studied the photos I'd taken of the tattoo on Jane Doe's thigh.

He handed the iPad back to me. "That is the work of Slade Teller. The wings have his initials inside one of the geometrics. Slade is an upfront guy. He'll want money, but if he doesn't know anything, he'll say so. I need to let him know when you'll be coming. You know, like having an appointment instead of just barging in."

"I'd like to talk to him today."

Dev laughed. "Patience isn't one of your strong suits, is it? Slade doesn't like talking on the phone. He's not keen on computers either. I have a friend who flies charters for a living. You can't afford him, but if he's got a client today, maybe you can deadhead with him. Can't promise when you'll get home. How bad do you want to find out about this dead girl?"

Apparently badly enough. "Call Slade," I said. "Ask him where I need to meet him and how I get from the airport to his office."

I was about ready to leave when Dev stopped me.

"A man come in here yesterday asking about a girl with a butterfly tattoo."

"Shit. How…"

"He said his daughter had a friend who had one, and he wanted to get his daughter the same one for her birthday. But her friend was missing. I mean, like that's bullshit even a cow would be ashamed of. He described Alicia and asked if I'd seen her. I told him I didn't do butterflies or young girls and he left. One girl with a butterfly on her ass is dead and some guy comes in looking for another girl that sounds like Alicia. Makes you wonder if your dead child and Alicia were friends, that maybe both got the same tat from Slade. Take Alicia's picture with you and see what he says, but everything points to Alicia being in serious trouble."

My original goal was to give the dead girl a name. Suddenly, I felt tasked with saving a living one.

When I didn't leave, Devin shrugged his shoulders. "What?"

"Do you remember a sailor hanging around my mother before I was born? His name might have been James."

He looked at me for a moment uncertainly. "Where did that come from?"

"Something I heard."

"A ship would dock and some of these guys would hit the local bars. Locals stayed clear of them most of the time. A few guys I knew liked to tangle with 'em, but I'd already had a taste of prison and stayed clear of that shit. You mother was really pretty, so I'm sure they hit on her. That's all I know. If anyone would remember, it would be Ethel. She watched her barmaids like a brood hen. Maybe you should ask her."

I said I would, even though it struck me as a really bad idea.

*****

It was just after 11:30 when I got a call from Devin to head for the airport. While waiting in the terminal, my phone rang again. This time is was Detective Murphy.

"What did I do this time?" I said.

"What amazes me is that you seem so smart, but when you open your mouth, you prove me wrong. Consider this a courtesy call. The arresting officer ran Tess's plates before pulling the paperwork for filing charges. This morning, he gets a hit on a missing person's report filed in New York by a man claiming to be her fiancé, a guy named Hank Bennet. I don't know any more than that, but it seems your girl skipped town without telling him where she was going. She's got no priors, so we can't arrest her. Maybe it's a lover's quarrel, or maybe he hit her, but she's got a story to tell. I know she's taking care of your mom. Just thinking you might want to talk to her sooner than later."

"I appreciate the call, Detective. I'll take care of it." The detective didn't hang up. "Was there something else?"

"No. It'll keep."

I slipped the phone back in my pocket. Tess said she had baggage. Now I knew his name.

*****

Fifteen minutes later, I climbed into a small plane, the first passenger aboard. Before anyone else came on, the door was closed, and the plane taxied down the runway. Moments later, it was over the water, banked sharply, and headed northward. As the plane gained altitude, I thought about how my life had become intertwined with the lives of two runaways — one dead and one in hiding — and with a young woman, educated and smart who was also running away from something or someone.

The news about Tess saddened me, partly, I will confess because I had entertained the notion of getting to know her better, but also because there was nothing I could do to help her. What her relationship was with her fiancé, what caused her to leave him, why he filed a missing person report — all subjects I'm certain Tess preferred not to discuss — would soon be raised by the police. In the best of all possible worlds, it was simply a lover's quarrel — something easily explained and quickly forgotten. But if I'd learned anything in the last few days, it was that life rarely takes the easiest, simplest path.

My thoughts were interrupted when the intercom suddenly popped on. A moment later, the cabin was filled by a crackly voice: "Good morning. I have a pickup in Palm Beach this afternoon. Dev asked if I could leave a bit early. Enjoy the flight."

As we made our way up the Keys, I imagined a young woman boarding a boat, eating caviar, and drinking a fancy alcoholic beverage, perhaps champagne. Maybe the day would have been like all others, or maybe something special had been planned. But somewhere before reaching Key West, the girl's life was stolen from her. Her body was dumped into the Gulf, food for bacteria and sea creatures, to be forgotten forever. Whether by chance or by fate, our paths had crossed. With a bit more luck, I would soon learn the dead girl's name.

CHAPTER SEVEN

To my surprise, awaiting me at the terminals was a man holding a card with my name written on it. The driver said he had been instructed to drop me off a few blocks away from Slade's salon, a precaution that seemed odd to me. I checked Slade's address on my phone, and followed the map instructions, passing what appeared to be a cluster of professional buildings. Slade, like Dev, operated without a store front, offering only expensive skin art to a clientele that wanted unique tattoos without being seen getting it.

I arrived at a small professional building fronted by a courtyard featuring a fountain in the middle. Under swaying palm trees and beside colorful tropical flowers, a dozen or so people on benches seemed to be waiting for others to emerge from the large sliding glass doors. Looking at the building directory, I quickly learned that if I needed a plastic surgeon, cosmetic dentist, or psychiatrist, I'd arrived at the right place. Curiously, there was no listing for Slade or his business.

I found the suite number Dev had given me and pressed what looked like a doorbell. A moment later, I heard a soft buzz and the snap of a magnetic door bolt. I opened the door and found myself in a small anteroom lit with soft indirect lighting and bathed in new-age music that seemed more appropriate for a yoga center than a tattoo parlor.

I expected Slade to enter the room in some kind of chic outfit, maybe leather pants and a skin jacket. The man who appeared from an invisible door was something else: a short, fat man in a T-shirt and plaid shorts that, to my taste, hung a bit low on his hips. He smiled, revealing a scattering of lonely teeth. I smiled back, but truthfully hoped he'd close his lips and keep them closed.

He offered me a bottle of water, then examined the photos on my iPad. I surmised from the occasional "yes" and "that's right" that he was intently engaged in a conversation with himself. The whole session took only a few minutes. "I remember. Two girls — teenagers — came to me as friends of a wealthy client — the wife of a famous actor, to be precise. I don't normally ink children, but sometimes..." Slade shrugged. "So, they wanted small butterflies on opposite thighs. Cute girls with perfect butts. I don't say that because I'm a pervert, but because the shape of the tissue can complicate an otherwise easy job. One of the girls was tall and the other short, perhaps a bit younger."

I showed him the picture of Alicia from the flyer.

"That's her. Her friend's name was Megan. I know that because my grandmother had the same name. Megan was a sad girl, as I remember. Alicia was trying to make her happy. But you know..."

"I'm sorry to say, but I think Megan is dead and Alicia is in trouble. If I could talk to the woman who sent them here..."

Slade raised his hands. "No way, man. You don't know who you're messing with, but I do." He stood up. "That's all I got to say. I think you should go."

"I'm sorry. I'm just trying to find out who Megan was, to tell her family what happened to her. Can you at least tell me her last name?"

Slade studied me for a moment. "Dev told me you were pushy. You tell him he owes me. Wait here." He exited the room, then returned with a photograph. "These are the two girls posing with their tats exposed. The lady who paid for the tats took the photo and gave me a copy. On the back, she wrote the girls' names: 'Megan Jones and Alicia Dorsett.' You can keep it. Just don't tell anyone where you got it. If you're smart, the picture will tell you what you want to know."

I reached for my wallet, but he waved me off. "Dev told me what you're up to. I'm glad to help bring that little girl some peace. I'm sure she didn't have much of it when she was alive. Just don't come back or tell anyone you were here. Word hits the street that I can't keep my yap shut, and I'm through."

Before I could ask any more questions, he opened the door to the suite and politely ushered me out.

*****

The car was waiting for me a few blocks from Slade's studio. I sat in the back and studied the photo. The girls were on a dock. The slips were mostly occupied by small, but expensive-looking boats. In the background was a large yacht, the word "cloud" visible on its stern.

When we stopped at a traffic light, I handed the photo to my driver. "Do you recognize the marina or the yacht in this picture."

He studied it for a few seconds and handed it back. "Everyone around here knows that yacht. It's the *My Cloud*, like in the song by the Rolling Stones. Rumor has it that Mick was with Giles

Horan when he bought the boat, but I doubt it. I don't see him as a Stones fan."

The name Giles Horan was vaguely familiar, but I had no idea who he was. My driver wasn't eager to fill me in.

"Mr. Horan is like a billionaire. But he don't like people to talk about him. Lots of stories about him, but …you can't believe everything people say about these rich guys, you know? People with an axe to grind start stuff and it gets around. I don't listen to it." He laughed. "Okay, I listen but I don't repeat it. Anyway, that's what I know." He glanced at me in the rearview mirror. "You have business with him?"

"No. Just curious how my nieces got so close to a big boat."

The driver laughed. "Girl wiggles a nice ass like that, and she can get anything she wants in this town."

*****

The Internet proved to be more informative. While Giles was a philanthropist associated with a long list of notable good deeds, another line of hits questioned whether he was a sexual predator and trafficker of young girls. An article purporting to have proof of these allegations had appeared several years ago in a Miami newspaper, only to be retracted a few weeks after publication as "a failure by the editors to verify unsupported allegations from questionable sources." The article's bylined reporters were fired, and the paper agreed to run an apology on its editorial page. After the paper's publicly humiliation, no other major media outlet would touch any stories alleging sexual improprieties by Giles Horan.

When I searched the yacht name, I was stunned by the third item that came up: "*My Cloud* docks at Serenity Key in Key West

70

for Fantasy Fest." I clicked on the link and was served a page that included a picture of the yacht and an excerpt from an article that was three days old:

> The *My Cloud* pulled into the dock on Serenity Key, the man-made island owned by Giles Horan that is home to his private resort, with a passenger list drawn from the country's rich and famous. The cruise, which originated from Palm Beach, cost each of the passengers a whopping $50,000, all of which will go to charity. The lucky passengers will stay on Serenity Key while having full access to all the Fantasy Fest Events.

I could read the rest of the article by buying a subscription to the publication, but I had read enough. The photograph of two girls standing on a dock yards away from Giles' yacht meant I had factual basis for associating them with the boat or with Giles Horan. I stared harder at the picture, a story forming in my head — a story about two young girls traveling on the boat of a rich man once credibly accused of sex trafficking, and the body of one of them, Megan Jones, found in the Gulf, a girl whose last meal was caviar. Whether the story had any truth to it, or if was just the fanciful product of someone eager to connect a small collection of dots was, at the moment, unknowable. The one person who could tip the balance either way was the other girl in the photograph — Alicia Dorsett. It was time we met.

CHAPTER EIGHT

For me, the photograph of the two girls, the rich man's yacht in the background, was more than just evidence. It represented a personal victory over a justice system with an institutionalized indifference toward marginalized victims. I couldn't bring justice to my murdered mother, but I had managed to give Jane Doe a name. I hadn't solved the case, but I might have found a key clue to where she had spent the last hours of her life.

Ninety minutes after leaving West Palm Beach, the small plane touched down at Key West Airport. On the way to my car, I dialed Detective Murphy's office phone, eager to share my news and accept whatever congratulatory words he might be willing to offer. Before I could explain where I'd been and what I'd learned, he made a shocking announcement: "Thanks for calling. I don't have but a few minutes, but the dead girl's death has been officially ruled an accident and the case closed. I may have mentioned that in accordance with local procedure, her body will be cremated, and her ashes deposited in a pauper's plot at a local cemetery. Your assistance in recovering the body and helping the officer at the scene are greatly appreciated. I apologize, but I have to go."

The line went dead. So much for my hero's moment.

I stood by my car staring at the phone. *An accident?* Megan lived fourteen years, only to disappear from the earth, a box of ashes deposited in a common grave without so much as a marker. I waited for the shock and anger to pass, but it didn't. Before I could call him back, I received a text confirming my reservation for three at Castro's Last Stand, a Cuban café close to Hemmingway's house, but rarely frequented by Anglos. I hadn't made a reservation, but I had an idea who had.

The Last Stand was located on Olivia Street. I drove to my house and parked my car, then walked to the café. A small white clapboard house with a wraparound veranda and a collection of mismatched tables and chairs, the place was as unpretentious as the food was authentic … *and* delicious. A short dark-haired man with a big toothy smile greeted me and led me to a table that couldn't be seen from the street.

As I approached, Tess stood up, a scowl on her face. "Do you know what's going on?" She glanced at Detective Murphy, who was sitting at the table, ignoring both of us. "The detective shows up, tells me we're going to meet you for dinner, and brings me here. Something's happened and I want to know what it is."

I sat across from Detective Murphy and tossed the picture of the two girls onto the table.

He was sitting in the shade fanned by a gentle breeze. Even so, a bead of sweat traced a line across his forehead. He looked pale and exhausted but forced a smile. "You've been busy," he said.

Tess sat next to me and stared at the picture.

"This is a photograph of Alicia Dorsett with a girl named Megan Jones," I said in a steady, calm voice. I tapped the picture with my finger. "See the butterfly tattoos? See that yacht behind them? That yacht belongs to Giles Horan. It's parked a mile or so from where we're sitting. I'd think the police would be interested in talking to the owner of that boat. But you tell me the case is closed. I'm confused, so why don't you unconfuse me?"

"What do you mean the case is closed?" asked Tess.

"Tell her, Detective."

A waitress arrived with a small pot, three small cups, and a tray of pastries. The cups were filled with a dark beverage topped with foam. "It's sweet and potent," said Detective Murphy. "The best Cuban coffee outside of Havana, though I warn you: It's an acquired taste."

I took a sip. The coffee was strong, but oddly smooth and satisfying.

Tess took a sip, made a face and set the cup down. "Someone tell me what the fuck is going on?"

Detective Murphy looked at her coldly. "Officially, the case is closed. Ruled an accident. Time to move on."

"Why would you close the case?" she asked.

"I didn't. In a manner of speaking, Jake did." The detective grabbed the photograph and waved it at me. "Piecing things together, it seems you showed someone this photo, after which the governor's office received a call from one of Giles Horan's lawyers. The lawyer claimed that his client's name was being unfairly associated with an incident in the Keys involving the death of a young woman. By the time you landed in Key West, Jane Doe's death was formally ruled an accident. I was informed that the case was closed, and I was to have no further contact with you."

His jaw tightened and his voice became loud and tense. "This is the shit amateurs cause. You got a lead and then you shared it with someone you didn't know. He could have been Giles' brother

75

for all you fucking knew. I'm sure he got paid handsomely for letting Giles know that some kid from Key West was asking about his yacht and two girls with butterflies tattoos."

"Her name is Megan — Megan Jones," I said, snatching the picture from his hand.

"There is no Megan Jones. Not now. You fucked up."

Tess sat back in her chair and folded her arms across her chest. "Giles Horan just snaps his fingers and Megan is erased from the planet?"

Detective Murphy slammed his fist on the table sending silverware flying and coffee spilling. "You think I'm pissed because Giles Horan screwed with my case? Get this through your thick heads: I warned you about playing cop. You, Missy, get yourself arrested, and Jake here gets the governor's ass kicked by one of Giles' lawyers. That shit flows downhill, to people like me. I swore to my supervisor I had no knowledge of what you two were doing, but I came close to getting suspended. This shit must stop, only it's too fucking late."

"What do you mean, *too late*?" I asked.

Detective Murphy poured himself another cup of coffee and took a sip. "You still don't get it. I'll explain it to you. The world is divided into two groups. You've got your average grunts who have to live by the rules — that's most of us. We know if we get caught doing something illegal, we're going to pay a price. Then there are people like Giles. Shit rolls off him because the people who make and enforce the rules always give him a pass."

He looked at Tess, then at me. "What? You think I'm making this up?" He shook his head. "You can't think I work in this god forsaken place because I like it. Until a few years ago, I had nice cushy job in Palm Beach. Had a girlfriend of sorts. Could get a good meal at an expensive restaurant on credit, if you follow my drift. Life was good. I was in Vice, and we were quietly building a case against Giles Horan for racketeering, raping a child, prostitution, pornography, and assorted other felonies. I had no clue who this guy was, except that, by all accounts, he was a rich scumbag. We had him dead to rights — even had an indictment drafted and ready to file. Then we previewed the case to the state attorney general, and it all fell apart from there. The identities of the abused girls were leaked to the press. Giles' attorneys hammered them, making them out to be prostitutes and drug queens. The local prosecutor was brought up before the state disciplinary agency on an ethics charge and disbarred. Some of the cops on the team were investigated by police Internal Affairs and had to get lawyers. Some were fired and others were demoted. My partner killed himself. I was publicly humiliated for allegedly using doctored photos and other such bullshit. I was lucky to make it to this backwater to kill time until my pension kicked in."

"Fuck," I said. "I just wanted to…"

Tess shook her head. "Horan can't control everyone."

"He can, and he does. But you still haven't fully grasped the shit you're in. Alicia is still in Key West, somewhere, or Giles thinks so. If she wasn't, Giles would have gone back to Palm Beach. He never stays the full week of Fantasy Fest. You were never supposed to find Megan's body. Now that you have, Giles has to deal with you, but first he has to deal with Alicia. She and Megan were friends. Now Alicia is hiding somewhere. Why would she do that? One possibility is that she knows something about how Megan died. Giles is thinking the same thing. Maybe she does and maybe she doesn't. But Giles . . . he's got no choice but to make certain she never talks to the police."

"You can't blame Jake for what happened…"

I disagreed. "When I showed that picture to the driver," I said, "I signed Alicia's death warrant. That's why it's too late."

"Now you get it. Congratulations." Detective Murphy sipped his coffee, winced, then wrapped his arms around his waist.

"Are you all right?" asked Tess.

"Not really." He took in a slow breath, held it, then exhaled slowly. "I suppose some of this is my fault. I told you to ask questions thinking that maybe that would speed things up. But the fact is you two need to understand that your lives have changed. Before Jake went to Palm Beach, you could work on your house, fish, do whatever you do to waste your life. Now, you have two choices. You can do nothing and hope Giles will leave you alone. He's a vindictive prick, so that's not likely. You can continue to look for Alicia and hope to find her before Giles does, knowing that Giles will come after Ethel, Tess, me and God knows who else. Giles won't let you win. He may keep you alive until you lead him to Alicia, or he finds her on his own, but sooner or later, he will take everything from you. The only way to protect yourself is to get enough on him that he'll leave you alone. That assumes Alicia will talk to you." Detective Murphy pursed his lips and shook his head. "Alicia's your only hope, but realistically, this doesn't end well for you."

The detective took a halting breath, then groaned. He looked at us, his lower lip quivering. "Let me be honest. I'm a coward at heart. I'm not the one you should look to for help. I mean, when it suited me, I bent the rules, but going out on a limb for the likes of you or a street urchin isn't in my DNA. I told you to ask questions because I didn't want to be bothered. Now you're fucked." He forced a laugh through clenched teeth. "But if it's any consolation, last evening a doctor told me that I'm fucked, too. We're all fucked."

"Meaning what?" I asked.

"I'm sorry," he said through clenched teeth. "It'll pass."

"Tell us," I said.

He wiped his face with a napkin. "I've felt pretty bad for a while now. I don't like doctors. Most are quacks looking to make a buck. But my quack left me a message that he wanted to talk with me in person. Doctors do that when they have bad news. So, I showed up, he sat me down, then told me that I had stage four or five pancreatic something or other — basically that I won't live to spend my pension after all. He said he was sorry, then left the room. Didn't even suggest I take two aspirin. I'm a dead man walking. The kicker to the story: For taking part in this conversation, they hit me with a co-pay. Imagine getting paid to tell someone they've run out of rope. He could have just sent me a text for all the difference it made. Anyway, enough about that."

"Jesus, Murphy," said Tess. "There must be…"

"That's enough of that. If we are all fucked, we might as well drink," he said. "How about a margarita? I'm buying to make up for being a prick."

He raised his hand and a waiter appeared and took the order.

"Shouldn't we have a plan?" asked Tess.

The detective shook his head. "I don't need one. For you guys, it's pretty simple. Find Alicia and quickly."

*****

An hour later, Detective Murphy announced that he wasn't feeling well and left, leaving Tess and me sitting in an awkward silence. I poured a cup of coffee I didn't want while Tess used a straw to play with the slush at the bottom of her margarita glass. A waiter asked if we wanted dinner. We ordered the special, Lechon Asado, a roasted pork dish with vegetables Cuban style. To anyone nearby, we were a couple out enjoying a meal on a warm fall night. Nothing more. Nothing less.

But we weren't alone. Seated at the table with us was a problem I had created. Detective Murphy was right. I had picked a fight with Giles Horan. Tess and Ethy had not.

"I think —"

Tess raised her hand. "Don't even start with your 'this-is-my-problem' blather. I don't need you to protect me. Hell, I don't want you to protect me. I have my own reasons to want Giles Horan publicly castrated, and no, I'm not going to discuss them with you. So, let's talk about what we're going to do to nail the son-of-a-bitch and not waste time playing 'protect the helpless female.'"

I leaned back in my chair. "*Helpless* isn't a word I would ever associate with you. Maybe feisty or irritating or pushy…"

"Thanks for sharing, but I'm serious. What exactly are we going to do? I mean, you don't even know for sure that Megan was on Giles Horan's yacht on the night she died, much less that he had something to do with her death. Detective Murphy says that Alicia is hiding out because she knows something, but that's just a theory. He paints this dire picture of Giles killing you, me, Alicia, your mom — but based on what? Let's assume that he's right, that Giles killed the investigation into Megan's death. We really don't know why. Before we panic, we need a lot more information. How do we get it?"

"I can call Don and have him run the drift analysis on Megan's body to see where she entered the water and what boats were nearby. That might tell us if Megan was on his yacht. Maybe we can also talk to the woman who took the photo. Slade said it was the wife of a famous actor."

"Which one? I mean, there's probably more than one."

"I don't know."

"Detective Murphy said you're already on Giles' radar. That can't be good."

"Probably not."

"Your mom, I mean Ethy, says you're broke and have no prospects for employment. How are you going to pay for this drift analysis thing? Don't you have to pay a lot for information?"

"I have special skills that allow me to work on my own schedule, so no, I'm not without prospects for employment. The pay is pretty good when there's work. I doubt that anyone will be doing boat maintenance during Fantasy Fest. I have a bit of savings left and a few doubloons that I can sell. I'll think of something."

Tess laughed. "This is so fucked up. We're picking a fight with a man who could buy Key West, and all we have are a few old Spanish gold coins and the hope you get work scraping barnacles off of boats?"

"I also fix props," I said defensively. "We'll figure it out."

The food arrived. While the waiter was putting our plates on the table, Tess took my hand. "You realize you haven't said anything about my hair."

"You know it's hard for guys to know the rules about what to say and what not to say." I shrugged. "It's short and, well, blonde."

"And?"

"It's cute. If it matters, I like it. But, to be clear, I liked it long and brown, too. So, if I'm not supposed to like it, I don't."

"You can be a chicken-shit sometimes, but I'm sure some girls find that appealing in a man."

With the first taste of the rich stew, the conversation turned from being broke and scared to how good the food tasted.

"If I had to pick a last meal," said Tess, "this would be it."

"Speaking of meals, Ethy is going to want dinner, and we're already late."

I placed a carryout order for another pork and vegetable plate, then asked Tess where she had parked.

"Detective Murphy drove me here. I'm afraid you're stuck with me."

*****

Tess and I found Ethy at the dining room table. She was drinking coffee and playing solitaire. I grabbed two beers and handed one to Tess. Other than a nod of her head, Ethy barely took notice of me, continuing on about some TV show in which a man with two families for ten years was finally caught because he bought wife number one the wrong perfume. While deep into an analysis of why she thought the wives should have caught on sooner, she stopped in mid-sentence and looked at us, a rare smile teasing at the corners of her mouth.

"I may be an old woman with a damaged brain, but even I can sense that something is going on with you two. I might like the idea that you're sleeping together, but I have a hunch it's about that body Jake found and that I'm not going to like what you're about to tell me. But tell me you will." She tossed the cards onto the table. "Let's hear it."

"We brought you dinner," I said, holding up a bag.

"I ate already. What's going on?"

To my surprise, Ethy let me walk through the facts without

82

interruption or even a judgmental look. She asked to see the photograph of the two girls showing off their tattoos and then asked which one was dead and which was missing. The picture seemed to captivate her as she studied it for a few minutes.

"So young," said Ethy tossing the photo onto the table. "You think this man, Giles Horan, abused them?" Ethy's voice cracked with the word "abused," while her eyes conveyed a maternal anger I hadn't seen before.

Tess nodded. "Probably, but we don't know for sure he's connected to Megan's death. That's what we're trying to determine. I mean, we think he is, but we need to prove it."

"Prove it to whom?" snapped Ethy. "For God's sake, when are you going to get it into your thick skulls that no one who matters gives a shit what happened. What good is the truth going to do you or anyone else if the police don't have the balls to do anything about it?"

I started to speak, but she cut me off. "I've got something to say — something that needs saying and has for a long time. Get me a beer and meet me on the lanai."

I couldn't recall seeing Ethy ever drink a beer. She turned out to be more a gulper than a sipper. "I know you think I didn't care what happened to your mother — how that shaped your life." Her eyes glistened. "I did. I just didn't know what to do about it. Maurice and I ran the bar. That's who we were. Your mom was a waitress who worked for tips. We were all low-class people who served tourists, wife-beaters, and rich guys cheap drinks and loud music. I raised two kids, one who's in prison for killing a guy and another who's living on food stamps in Orlando. That was hard for Maurice — knowing that his kids were losers. It was hard for me, too. I coped by focusing on the business. Maurice took to chasing treasure ships. Then your mom gets pregnant, and he comes to her rescue. I mean, her situation seemed to bring him to life. It was too much for me. I resented her. Four years later, she was murdered, leaving me with a head full of guilt for being a bitch, and leaving you an orphan. With your mom gone, I resented you."

"Ethy…"

"Let me finish! Outside of Maurice, no one cared much because your mom was white trash, just like the rest of us. But he brought you to stay with us. You were four. You were a sad little boy, but you didn't mope about. Everyone at the bar supported you, except me. I'm sorry. I couldn't handle it. I resented you because you were smart, self-sufficient, and kind — everything my kids weren't. When you got older, you started asking questions about your mother. Maybe I could have stopped you from being obsessed with her murder, but I didn't. I suppose I took some pleasure in your misery." She tapped the picture of Megan and Alicia. "I don't want you to go through that again. I don't. But part of me wants you to help those girls, even though I know it's dangerous."

"If we pursue this, it may not be safe for you here," I said.

Ethy pushed back from the table. "My head exploded here while I was watching TV. It's not safe for me anywhere. Now, I'm going to bed. Do what you need to do. Just don't make me sorry I encouraged you."

Tess and I sat quietly, stunned by a woman I thought I knew, but clearly didn't.

"Don't ask me what that meant, because I don't want to talk about it," I said.

She picked at the label on the beer bottle, occasionally glancing at me.

"If you have something to say, you might as well do it now," I said.

She looked at me, started to speak, then hesitated.

"Say it."

She smiled at me. "I like you."

"No conversation that starts with those three words ever ends well. So, what's the *but*?"

"I think you like me, too, but I don't want you to get any ideas. I'm not reliable."

"If I wanted reliable, I'd have a dog or eat fiber cereals. You're smart and attractive and quirky, all of which I find interesting."

"You think I'm attractive?"

"I think lionfish are attractive. I'm aware that pretty things can hurt you if you don't understand what makes them tick. So, we're good. I'll see you tomorrow, and we can talk more about things then."

*****

When I arrived at my house, I was greeted by the smell of unpainted drywall compound and fresh cut lumber. Electrical wires dangled from holes in the walls and ceiling. My plan was to do as much of the work myself, paying only for the tasks that required special skills or were simply too labor intensive to be done alone. Progress was extremely slow, and the renovation seemed endless. At times, I found the chaos exciting. Tonight, it was exhausting.

I called Don and told him I didn't have the money to pay for the drift analysis, but I needed it right away. I offered to work for him for six months for free, but he ignored me.

"The body you found — it was a young girl?"

"Thirteen or fourteen."

"Sexually assaulted?"

"Repeatedly."

I heard Don groan. "I may be able to cut you some slack on the cost of the analysis. I'll get back to you."

I lay on the mattress, unable to fall asleep, my thoughts revisiting the events of the day without any coherent purpose. The mice in the attic were also apparently finding sleep difficult, only they were probably enjoying their waking moments more.

DAY 4

WEDNESDAY, OCTOBER 21

CHAPTER NINE

Morning was announced by crowing roosters and barking dogs. The sunlight teased my eyes and drew me from my troubled sleep. I made myself a breakfast of coffee, eggs, toast, and sausage and ate while immersed in self-deception, convincing myself that despite the events of yesterday, today would be measurably better. Perhaps things weren't as bad as Detective Murphy had suggested. Maybe Rachael would change her mind and arrange a meeting with Alicia. Or maybe Tess and I would meet with Giles on his yacht and come to an understanding that was good for everyone. These delusions, transparent as they may have been, were momentarily comforting.

Reality returned with the arrival of a large black car in my driveway and the rapping of a determined hand on my screen door. With the arrival of uninvited company, comfort gave way to fear that momentarily paralyzed me. The screen door rattled again. With one voice in my head screaming at me to grab a knife and another telling me to be calm, I walked to the door and confronted a middle-aged man with a broad grin and steely blue eyes.

"You're Jake Savage, right?"

"Who's asking?"

"Quite right. That's what you should ask when a stranger comes to your door." He flashed a smile. "But I already know that you are indeed Jake Savage so my question was part good manners and part rhetorical."

I started to close the front door when the man opened the screen door.

"You have no idea what I'm talking about. That happens, of course, because I think about everything so intensely that I forget other people can't hear what I'm thinking. I'm sure that's happened to you as well. Perhaps it would be helpful if I started at the beginning. My name is André Mitchell. The reason I'm here is that we have to talk about our mutual interest in Alicia Dorsett, something she stole, and the dead child named Megan."

"How do you know about Alicia and Megan?"

"I'm paid to know."

Before I could shut the front door, André was pushing inside. I stepped back and pulled out my phone.

"I see that we've gotten off on the wrong foot. If I came here to hurt you, I would have done it already. We're just going to chat. Whoever you were planning on calling won't get here before we're done. Please, put the phone down, relax and let's chat like the civilized people we are."

He walked past me; a smile seemingly etched permanently on his face.

"Now this is a project a young man could be proud of," he said scanning the living room. "You start with an open space. Then you put up the framing. But when that drywall goes up…Wow! Right? That feeling is sweet. Still more to be done but very nice."

I glanced at a drywall hammer.

88

"Don't do that. Seriously. Shooting you is the last thing I came to do, so don't give me cause."

"What about Alicia? How do you know about Megan?"

André turned to me. "Do you have coffee? I really like discussing important matters over a cup of something hot. Black is fine." He headed into the kitchen and I followed. "Now this is right out of the fifties. If it were in better shape, I'd say keep it. Sadly, it has to go, but might I suggest you stick with the retro look?"

He ran his finger over a chair, inspected it, then sat down. "Yes. Now, as to Megan, she was in this morning's newspaper — page twelve or thereabouts. A few column-inches. Wasn't news to me, but now everyone knows that an unidentified girl was found in the Gulf. The report says she died in a boating accident. Strangely, they didn't give her name. Actually, who cares what happens to the have-nots of the world? I find that sad." He made a point of looking me in the eyes. "I'm sure you do as well." He looked around the room. "This house is where your mother died. Now you live here. Some might find that odd."

"I think you should leave."

"Oh, I'm sorry. Your mother's murder still hurts. I paid a lot to get her case file. Seems like a half-assed investigation. Now that's something we can agree on."

I turned my back on him, denying him what pleasure he might get from seeing my hands shake, and poured him a cup of coffee. With a smile, I handed him the cup and watched as he inspected the papers strewn over the kitchen table.

"How about you tell me what you want," I said.

"Absolutely. No time to waste when you have real important business to deal with. Sit and let's chat. Before we start, I'm sure you've noticed I talk a lot without saying much. I was told it's a form of Turrets, but who knows?"

I sat across from him and waited.

"You're thinking that I work for Giles Horan." He took a sip of coffee. "This is very good. Light roast. Perhaps a bit too long in the pot, but good. Anyway, you'd be wrong; and you're wrong because you don't know what happened to get Megan killed and why Alicia is in hiding. Sadly, I can't tell you because then you'd know who my client is and that would cause problems. But now you understand that Giles isn't the only one interested in Alicia. That's important data for someone trying to decide how to conduct himself going forward."

"Back up. What exactly do you do?"

He gave me a bemused look. "Of course. You've never encountered someone like me. I'm a specialist of sorts. Actually, I'm one of a very few in my line of work. Think of me like one of those companies that comes in after a kitchen fire and makes everything look like it had been before. Only, my clients have committed a crime of some kind, or maybe killed someone and botched the cover up. This was probably not the career I thought I would have when I was five and was asked what I wanted to be when I grew up, but it's good money, and I'm really very good at it, usually, but this situation is pretty unique."

What was clear was that André wanted something. He also knew the answers to a lot of my questions. I could be afraid of him, which I was, or I could accept that killing me wasn't on his agenda and try to learn something from him.

He waved his cup at me. "Could you spare a bit more coffee?"

I freshened André's coffee and filled mine. "So, you were

hired to clean up a crime involving Megan," I said, returning to my seat. "The article said it was an accident. Seems like the newspaper got it wrong."

André pursed his lips and tilted his head slightly. Wagging a finger at me, he said, "You see? I think I'm smart and yet I've told you something you might not have known. Over-confidence is a problem I always have to guard against. But you? I'll have to watch you like a hawk, which actually I'm doing anyway."

"You said this situation was unique?"

André sipped his coffee, then folded his hands and rested them on the table. "When a mistake is made, the parties involved have a common interest in rectifying it. Most of the time, the way the problem is resolved makes no difference. But once in a while, the parties see the solution differently. They all want the problem resolved, but they don't want to be disadvantaged by the solution. In this case, a problem has arisen that affects several important people, albeit differently, each of whom has the power to independently find and hire a person like me. I hope that makes sense. Sometimes I ramble on, and after my last mistake, I'm being very careful. Just think of me as a guy who fixes messes."

"Your client wants to cover up the murder of a young girl in a particular way. How does that involve me?"

"I think you're jumping to conclusions." He clenched a fist and pressed it to his lips. "Okay, I'm going to break a rule and tell you that my client *didn't* kill anyone and believes that the proof of his innocence involves something Alicia stole. Dear me! I hope I didn't say too much. Oh well, another horse has left the barn. If I talk to you much longer, the barn will soon be empty!"

"You work for someone who didn't kill Megan, but needs something Alicia stole to prove it? Because someone wants to frame him for the killing?"

"I want to be careful with you because you're a smart guy, and you may trick me into revealing something more. So, let's just say that my client, could be a man, could be a woman, wants the object Alicia stole but has no interest in hurting Alicia."

"What object?"

"A laptop computer."

I stared into André's eyes and laughed. "I think I get what you're saying. The people involved in this crime want to protect themselves, but don't give a rat's ass about Megan. If this computer can prove who didn't kill Megan, presumably it can also prove who did."

André continued to smile, but his eyes revealed a growing impatience. "I sense you're getting distracted. You're thinking of the body of the young girl — Megan — you found in the Gulf. I believe you've connected Megan and Alicia to each other and to Giles Horan. In your mind, you want someone to pay for what happened to Megan. That's because you're a noble sort who wants bad people to rot in hell for eternity. I will put it to you bluntly: Your goal, which I thoroughly understand and even admire, will fail and will probably — no, most certainly — get you killed. What does that accomplish? Nothing! But if you can recover the object and bring it to me, my client can protect Alicia and you from the others. Hell, I'd even bring in some contractors and finish up your house for free, maybe leave enough cash hidden in a closet so you can do whatever you want for a long time."

"You want me to find the laptop Alicia stole and give it to you so Giles doesn't find it first."

"That's perfect. Keep in mind that Giles will probably kill Alicia for stealing it. It's in his nature. You give it to me, and I will protect her and you."

92

"And Megan's murder is just forgotten?"

"Sadly…"

"What if I say no?"

His permanent smile morphed into a momentary scowl marked by a flash of anger. The scowl quickly receded, and André's pleasant demeanor returned. He stood up and gulped down his coffee. "Great chat," he said, walking to the door. "I'll be in touch."

The black car carrying the enigmatic André Mitchell backed out of my driveway. I watched as it disappeared from view, only vaguely aware of how much trouble I was in.

*****

Tess sat at my kitchen table, her hands wrapped around a can of diet soda, her normally happy face distorted by lowered eyebrows and downturned lips. She sipped her soda and listened while I summarized what André had conveyed to me an hour before, her eyes occasionally darting to a collection of maps and charts strewn on the table.

"He really said that if you tried to find out what happened to Megan, he would kill you?"

"No. He said I would die. Whether André would do the killing or someone else wasn't explicitly stated. He also admired the remodeling work."

Tess threw her hands into the air, splashing a bit of soda onto the table. "That makes me feel so much better."

I filled a glass with water. "I'm just telling you what he said."

"But he admitted that Megan was murdered, or so it sounds."

"He talked in circles, like a dog trying to lie down but never actually doing so. The message was that if we want to save Alicia, we need to find the laptop she stole and give it to him. In exchange for the laptop, his client will protect Alicia and me from Giles."

"Do you believe him?"

"All I know for sure is that he showed up here looking for me. The rest...hell, I don't know. We have to assume that if we go looking for Alicia, we'll be watched by André and probably Giles, which, of course, puts everyone we talk to at risk. Maybe that's the game. We lead André to Alicia, and he whacks all of us."

From the table, Tess picked up a nautical map showing the waters around Key West. A series of lines emanated from a small circle, diverging as they curved northwesterly. "What's this about?" she said.

"Each of the blue lines projects a path by which Megan's body could've arrived at the spot where I found it. The lines reflect variations in the estimated time of death."

"These red lines, what are those?"

"Those lines show the course taken by all the larger boats that passed through those waters a few hours before and after she died. The dashed line is the course taken by Giles Horan's boat on its cruise from Palm Beach to Key West."

She studied the map, then looked at me. "The dashed line is pretty close to two of the projections."

"I think it proves that Megan went into the water from his boat, which is where Megan was murdered," I said. "Of course, his lawyer would disagree."

Tess tossed the map back onto the table. "A man shows up in a black car, waltzes into your house, and basically says that if you want to save Alicia, you have to find a laptop she stole, but doesn't tell you how to go about it. He also explains, nicely, that looking into Megan's death will get you killed. You're take is that we can't look for Alicia or the laptop without potentially leading André or someone else to Alicia and we can't look into Megan's death without getting ourselves killed. Is that about right?"

I nodded. "Close enough."

Tess pushed a lock of hair out of her eyes. "This is pretty fucked up."

"One more thing," she said. "Detective Murphy called. He's arranged for us to have lunch in Marathon with an ex-cop named Roy who investigated Giles Horan a few years back. I'm not sure I see the point if we aren't interested in what happened to Megan. Surprised me that he'd bother after ripping us to shreds last night, but he's an odd duck. Sad about him dying."

Tess took a deep breath, then expelled the air with a slow hiss. "Why is everything so complicated?"

The question begged for an answer, but all that came to mind were platitudes. I poured the last of the coffee into my cup and put it in the microwave. "Rationally, we should back down, go back to what we were doing before Megan floated into my life, and move on. I don't think I would be judged too harshly for making that decision. Hopefully, Giles and André would tire of us and everything would just go back to normal."

The microwave signaled that the coffee was hot. I took it and sat across from Tess. "But some things just bug me to the point where good judgment isn't relevant. Maybe it's my mom's murder, maybe it's dealing with the bullies in school, maybe I just have a wire loose. No matter what Giles or André or Murphy says, what I want more than anything else is to knock that smug, shit-eating grin from Giles' fucking face. Maybe it's not so complicated after all."

Tess drained her soda, then pressed her fingers into the empty can until it clanked in protest. "I'm afraid of a few things. I don't like spiders, I'm not fond of creepy multi-legged insects, and I don't want to die of some really debilitating disease. But what I fear the most is growing old and bitter, of being consumed by regret. It stalks me, like the monster that hides under your bed when you're a kid. Despite my best efforts, I have already accumulated a sizable stash of things I'd like to do over. If I walk away from Megan and Alicia knowing what Giles will do to other thirteen- and fourteen-year-old girls, how am I going to feel when I look back at my life? What if I have a daughter? What do I tell her about what I decided to do now? I don't want to die, but I don't want to hate myself either. That choice sucks, but that's where I'm parked."

"Kind of binary," I said.

"I want to see Giles Horan's yacht. I want to see where this man hangs out."

"That won't be easy, but I might know someone who can help us. As to lunch with Detective Murphy, we have to eat anyway, right? We can talk to his friend, Roy... see what he knows. We can't go to the shelter, but we might be able to get a message to Rachael Hackett to meet us and talk to us about Alicia. I'll ask Clara Morse if she can help arrange that. From here on out, we have to be careful, even if that means being paranoid. Take small steps and see where they lead us."

Tess nodded. "Small steps."

The problem with steps of any size is that it's hard to know when you've gone one step too far.

CHAPTER TEN

The Key West harbor is located on the north side of the island. Adjacent to the ferry terminal is a large marina where dozens of large and expensive yachts are anchored. Giles' *My Cloud*, unfortunately, was not one of them. Getting a view of that boat would require a visit to his private key, which in turn required someone with enough social weight to get past Giles' private security detail.

I had worked on a number of the boats moored in the marina, including a fifty-footer called *The Insider*. The person I was looking for was its owner, Kaye Jacobs, a retired schoolteacher who, at the age of fifty, made a killing on three stocks no one was paying attention to. Part of her fortune was given to lawyers who successfully defended her against allegations of insider trading. She paid taxes on the rest, quit her job, and bought a boat big enough to live and party on. To my knowledge, she couldn't drive the boat herself and wasn't keen on venturing far from land. Every few weeks, she'd hire someone to take the boat out to keep the engines clean and to use up the fuel before it went stale. Otherwise, the boat and Kaye stayed put.

Tess and I found her on the aft deck, a Bloody Mary in her hand and a bag of ice on her head. She stood up, sending the icepack flying. "Did we have something scheduled for this morning," she shouted, "because if we didn't, I'm not taking visitors at the moment!" She rubbed her temples. "That wasn't friendly. On second thought, come on up. How about a beer?"

We declined the beer but accepted water with lemon. "If I didn't hire you, what brings you to my floating abode?"

"Short or long version?" I asked.

"Start short. If I don't barf up breakfast and my curiosity is piqued, we can fill in the details."

"We want to see Giles Horan's yacht or, better yet, get on it," I replied. "I was thinking you might be able to help."

Kaye closed her eyes. "Fuck. That's funny. If my head didn't hurt, I might be laughing my ass off. No, of course I can't get you near or on that fucker's yacht. What, you think my piddly millions have earned me a ticket to Giles World? Not that I'd go if it did."

"Any particular reason you don't like him?" asked Tess. "I mean, have you met him?"

Kaye took a sip of her drink and made a face. "Looks like it's time to switch to coffee. Take a seat at the table." She spun around, almost fell, then disappeared below deck.

"She's different," said Tess. "I kind of like her."

"I know, but we're wasting our time."

Tess shrugged. "We can hear what she has to say. Besides, I'm not sure we have anything pressing to do."

Kaye reappeared with a tray of coffee and pastries that looked like baklava. "This Greek man sends me these every few months. He tells me he's in love with me, but I know he just wants my money." She shrugged. "I may have agreed to marry him, but I don't remember. That was a few months ago. After a while down here, every day feels the same." A smile exploded on her face. "And so does every man!"

She poured coffee, curled up in a chair, and said: "Where to start? Let me ask you, what do you know about Giles Horan?" Before I could respond, she raised her hand. "The answer is nothing. You want to pick a fight with an enemy you don't know. That's not smart, but I'm not here to be judgmental."

"We never said we wanted to pick a fight," said Tess.

"You didn't have to, honey. What did he do? Grope you? Give you drugs and rape you? Nothing would surprise me." Kaye was still smiling, but the joy had left her voice. "I was on Giles' yacht with a man I'll call Brian, who was the CEO of a big company. Giles approached Brian with an offer to invest in one of Dillon Farrell's films. Dillon is one of Giles' properties. He uses him to entice rich and famous people wanting to hang out with movie stars and to convince teenaged girls he can get them acting jobs. Anyway, Brian said no, politely at first. When the offer was repeated, Brian declined a bit more emphatically. I could see that Giles wasn't someone who liked to be rebuffed. A bit later, I was invited to take a tour of the lower deck and offered a glass of champagne. Twenty minutes later, I was on my back, unable to move. Giles was hovering over me, twirling my panties on his index finger. My brain was commanding me to flee, but I couldn't move."

"Jesus! What happened?" asked Tess.

"Not what you think. Apparently, the yacht's running lights were on the fritz and the officers on a harbor patrol boat were making noises about boarding the yacht. Giles left and Brian came to my rescue."

"We think a young girl may have been killed on his yacht a few nights ago," I said.

"When I'm speaking coherently, don't interrupt me. Where was I? Yes. There are two man-made islands in the harbor. One is Sunset Key and the other is Wisteria. Sunset has private homes and cottages. Wisteria is home to squatters. Giles tried to buy Wisteria, but a lawsuit between the federal government and a family claiming to own the island made that impossible. He couldn't buy one, so he made one using material dredged from a portion of the main harbor channel. The dredging was the passion project for a group of businessmen who wanted to attract larger cruise ships to Key West.

"Environmentalists joined with long-time residents to oppose the project. The harbor is in the Florida Keys National Marine Sanctuary, meaning a full environmental impact statement was going to be required. Before that, a feasibility study from the U.S. Army Corps of Engineers was needed. Battle lines were drawn, and a political fight ensued. You had letters to the editor, public debates, money going to PACs on both sides — a dog fight to say the least. Suddenly, Giles offered to pay for a channel project in exchange for getting waivers on dozens of state and federal regulatory requirements.

"He got his island. Buried in all the paperwork were tax deferments that lasted twenty years. You don't accomplish something of that magnitude by handing out free cruises and presidential suites to well-connected people. You succeed because you own them, because you have perpetual leverage over them, because you can destroy them if they fail to please you. Giles could murder someone in the middle of Duval Street with a hundred witnesses and no one would care."

"Did you file a complaint against him?" asked Tess.

"No, sweetie, I did not. But Brian invested a sizable amount of money in a Dillon Farrell film to make sure videos of me sucking Giles' cock didn't make it to the Internet. Shit happens. Now eat up. If I'm left with all of this pastry, I'm just going to eat it and my boobs are big enough already. You, sweetie, you could use a bit of filling out."

She stuffed a pastry in her mouth and licked her fingers. "That is really good. Anyway, so here's a bit of trivia for you. I considered buying that yacht before Giles got his hands on it. Ten million was about my limit, but I could afford it. Then I start thinking about what I'd do on a hundred-and forty-foot boat with all those bedrooms and sitting areas. Before you know it, family and old friends start thinking they can spend the winter with you. I loved the master bedroom on the main deck — great panoramic views. But in the end, I settled for this tugboat, which is also more than I need. I can show you the brochure if you want."

Before I could respond, Kaye was out of her chair and below deck.

"For a woman with a hangover, she's mighty chatty," said Tess.

"To be polite, we'll look at that brochure for a few minutes, but then we have to go."

Tess gave me one of her patented smirks. "You're uncomfortable around her. Oh my God, have you…"

"No, but she hits on me when I'm working for her. Kind of creepy. She pays well, but some services…"

"You know we may need the money. Just sayin'."

Kaye returned. We gawked at pictures of large wood-panel sitting areas, bars with marble tiled floors, and kitchens with granite counter tops. "That's the elevator to the lower and upper decks," she said, pointing at glass door. "More water? Coffee?"

101

Tess declined. Then, to my relief, she offered a plausible reason why we needed to leave.

As we made our way to the stern, Kaye looked at me. "Funny, I didn't know you were married. Sometimes, when you were working on the boat, I got an itch that I thought you might scratch, but I guess I was barking up the wrong tree."

"We're not married. Tess is actually engaged…"

The color drained from Tess's face. She said the words "excuse me" and hurried away.

"Wow. Look what I did," said Kaye. "You better go fix whatever is broken."

I caught up with Tess just beyond the pier. I reached for her arm, but she pulled it away, then turned and faced me.

"Leave me alone. I … don't…want…to…discuss it. Okay? What you said was unforgivable. How dare you presume to know…"

"You mean like asking where I found my dead mother? I presume to know because we have been stepping in and out of each other's space a lot lately. You got arrested. Your fiancé reported you missing. I'm tired. I blurted out something I shouldn't have. Truth be told, I'm worried about you. I'm just not doing a good job of showing it."

She made a fist, hit me lightly in the chest a few times, then pressed her head against my shoulder. I wrapped my arms around her and listened as she sighed away her anger.

"I couldn't do it," she said finally. "I thought I could. Hank is a great guy. He's on track to be partner at the firm where I worked. He makes me laugh. We have great friends. Everything a girl should want. At a big party we attended together, he asked me to marry him. I said yes. I wanted to want to marry him. But when the party ended, I didn't. I had a panic attack, the first of many."

She took a deep breath and then stepped back. "Hank wanted kids, a big apartment overlooking Central Park, a BMW…He wanted to live his life in one place surrounded by a collection of certain people. The more he talked about his plans, the more it sounded like a prison sentence for me. I was born restless. I was born to travel. We made plans to pick out rings and set a date, and I threw up. He'd talk about our honeymoon and my stomach would do cartwheels. Everyone in the firm thought we were the perfect couple. The whole thing was a lie."

She laughed as tears streamed down her cheeks. "The longer it went on, the more trapped I felt. I couldn't tell him because I didn't want to hurt him. I didn't want to marry him because I didn't want to be miserable for the rest of my life. So, one day, I packed my things, submitted my resignation, and just got in my car and started driving. I drove until I got here. I can't tell you how liberating it immediately felt to be so far from New York. In no time, I was in sync with the rhythm of this place. I signed up as an Uber driver and talked to people from everywhere and nowhere. I love the languages and dialects and cuisines. Then I met you and Ethel. I see a lot of me in you. Maybe that doesn't feel like a compliment…Anyway, here we are."

I wiped a tear from her cheek. "Two peas in a pod."

She put her hand on my cheek. "Promise me this: No matter what happens between us, you won't put that kind of pressure on me."

Before I could answer, she pressed her lips to mine, let them linger for a few moments, and then walked away.

Life had served up another surprise, and quite a pleasant one at that.

CHAPTER ELEVEN

The lunch meeting with Detective Murphy was scheduled for two in the afternoon. Tess and I left Key West before one, stopping several times to see if we were being followed. By the time we arrived in Marathon, we had identified five cars that might be following us, none of which we saw more than once. The search for suspicious cars, while unlikely to be productive, consumed our time together, allowing us to avoid any further discussion of Tess's situation with Hank or her relationship with me. Ultimately, we agreed that the odds of us detecting a tail were zero or less and just headed to the restaurant.

The Sandpiper Café was about a mile off the main highway. A few minutes on a rough, shell and gravel road made us doubt Google Maps, but ultimately the directions proved accurate. A waiter led us to the end of a pier that extended about two hundred feet into the water and pointed to a table marked "RESERVED."

As the first to arrive, we ordered beers and took seats under a brightly colored umbrella. The table offered a view of an endless expanse of light blue water that blended into the sky at the horizon. White puffy clouds floated overhead. A lazy day, I thought. A day for sitting in a hammock or snorkeling above a reef. A day soon to be ruined by talk of Giles Horan and the murder of Megan Jones.

The waiter brought our beers and a bowl of conch fritters. "I could get used to this," said Tess.

The waiter nodded. "The beautiful blue water has tempted a lot of people. But it takes a special person to live here. Island living isn't for everyone. Most people who land here are running away from something. They never stick." He smiled. "Except me, of course. I'll never go back."

Two beers later, I watched as Detective Murphy and a short, muscular man whom I presumed was ex-Detective Roy Perching, approached us. If Detective Murphy looked perpetually tired, Roy looked permanently pissed off. He had the scowl of a bulldog and held his arms out like a man ready for a fight.

After being castigated by Detective Murphy the night before, I wasn't certain what another meeting was supposed to accomplish. On the other hand, I hadn't been blessed with a burst of inspired thought as to how to resolve the problems with Alicia, André, and Giles. At worst, Tess and I would be subjected to another lecture on the perils of sticking our noses where they didn't belong. At best, Roy would announce that he was going to board Giles' yacht, shoot him, and set the boat on fire. What occupied the middle of those possibilities I couldn't imagine.

My assessment of Roy as a gruff, snarly, combative man was contradicted when he stopped a waiter who gave him a quick man-hug. A burst of laughter followed, and the two men parted all smiles.

"I ordered four sandwich platters and two more beers," said Roy, offering me his hand. "I'm Roy Perching. My friends call me Perch. You can call me Roy." He laughed. "Just goofing with you. Murph says you have no sense of humor, but he says that about me, too. That's because he's an old fart who wouldn't know a joke if you hit him with it."

Murphy took his seat. Ignoring Roy, he said, "I thought it would be good to get to know each other and get on the same page."

Roy picked at the fried conch plate. "We don't have to rehash what we already know. Murph tells me that you want to pin a murder on Giles Horan. To be clear, I'd like nothing more than to see that asshole sent to prison, where he could find love in all the wrong places. But the fact is, you start messing with Giles and you'll be bringing up a lot of old news most people, including me, would prefer to forget. I was a detective back before Giles took a hatchet to my career. Now I'm a glorified security guard. I actually make more money, but being a detective was a job I loved. Murphy will tell you he hates his job, but he didn't use to. All that is to give you context for why I'm reluctant to help you. Still, I'd like to hear what you know and see if we might get creative."

I looked at Detective Murphy, then at Roy. "We could have had this little chat on the phone. I mean, if all we're going to do is have a sandwich and a few beers and shoot the shit about Giles, it's a total waste of time."

Roy shook his head. "Murph said you were an impatient sort. Me? I like to get to know someone a little before I decide to put my ass on the line for them."

I started to speak, but Roy cut me off with a finger pointed at my face. The scowl returned and his face turned bright pink. "You're a kid who kicked a hornet's nest and is now looking for someone to save him. You owe us the courtesy of listening, even if we repeat the same bitter story. So, here's what went down. My department took a lot of shit for the Giles case, as if somehow, we'd screwed up the investigation.

"But the truth is that we had that prick dead to rights. We had witnesses. We had statements. We had a case that a first-year

107

law student could win. The prosecutor, Jamel Bryant, was a good attorney and a good guy. Then stories came out that he'd cheated his clients when he was in private practice. It was a hatchet job, plain and simple. He was pulled from the case and the new prosecutor was a piece of work. She started picking at our witness list, saying some of them weren't credible.

"Then she said our timeline was wrong because Giles' attorneys produced a diary and his private plane logs that showed Giles wasn't in town on certain dates. We used the press to get more witnesses, but then Giles sued the newspapers and got the reporters fired. In the end, Giles got off and Jamel offed himself. I was forced into early retirement. Now the two of you think you can tie him to a murder. You could have a hundred eyewitnesses and it wouldn't matter."

"Murphy said as much," I said.

"So, we give up?" asked Tess.

Roy drained his beer and wiped his mouth on his forearm. "If you're smart, you would." He raised his hands, palms outward. "Okay, that wasn't fair. Let's cool our jets. Tell me what you know, and we'll start over."

I went through the evidence as I understood it, concluding by showing Roy the computer simulation of where Megan's body went into the water.

Roy studied the map for a moment. "Looks like a hurricane spaghetti plot," he said. "I'm impressed. Shit like this is expensive, but it's not enough. Giles' lawyer will argue that Megan was hiding on the boat and just fell off. Before you get all pissy, I'm not saying what you have isn't helpful. But what you need is to prove Megan was invited onto the yacht, that Giles knew she was there, and that he knew something happened to her."

Detective Murphy leaned forward. "Roy and I were talking about how going straight at Giles is pointless. He will just raise the ante, and then all you'll be doing is reacting. He'll control the conversation. We have to set him on his heels, make him think about settling. He's never compromised, so it would be a new experience for him."

I retrieved the nautical maps. "I'm not following."

"Neither am I," added Tess.

Roy shrugged. "It's simple. Go back to what André said about different people having different reasons to find Alicia. The key to Megan's murder is that laptop Alicia stole. Something on that computer tells us who did what on the night Megan was dumped into the Gulf. We need to find it, or make Giles think we did."

"So, you're back to finding Alicia," said Detective Murphy.

I shook my head. "We've been down that path with no luck. The locals who might know something won't say. Giles is offering money to the kids on the street."

"What if we could talk to someone on that boat the night Megan died?" asked Tess. "Someone who might be able to talk to Alicia in a way that we can't?"

For a moment, Roy and Detective Murphy exchanged glances. A smile grew on Roy's face. "There's one person who might be able to help."

Detective Murphy shook his head. "Please tell me you're not thinking about Lydia Carlson."

Roy grunted a short, amused laugh. "Lydia knows who is coming and going at Giles' compound. She has a source on the inside. Just depends on whether she's in a mood to share."

"This is a bad idea," said Detective Murphy. "I don't like it."

"I'll bite," I said. "Who is Lydia Carlson?"

The food arrived and the question went unanswered. The sandwiches were as messy as they were tasty. Roy, Tess, and I dug in, leaving our hands greasy and small clumps of fish on our faces. Murphy took a few bits, picked at his fries, and contented himself with sipping his beer. Tess and I followed our sandwiches with a large slab of key lime pie, then ordered coffee to mitigate the effects of a food coma.

While we devoured dessert, Roy folded his arms across his chest and maneuvered a toothpick around his mouth with his tongue. "How to describe Lydia Carson? By day, she's a real estate broker. Very successful. Gets her into lots of posh neighborhoods. When she's done fleecing rich people, she makes documentaries about corruption. Most of them are about little things — someone taking money from the animal shelter or stealing food from a food bank. The videos are quite good at exposing people. Some say she's nuts, others say she's just bitter and lonely. I find her tolerable in small doses and helpful when she wants to be."

"So, how does that help us?" asked Tess.

"Lydia was one of our sources when we first went after Giles. She provided us witnesses and gave us leads to follow. When the case went south, she took it pretty hard. About six months ago, Lydia turned her attention to the sex trafficking of young girls. That's when she decided to go after Giles Horan again. She posted flyers asking girls forced into sexual relations by Giles to come forward. Then she started showing up outside his compound and photographing his visitors. For all the people he's destroyed in his life, he can't seem to lay a glove on Lydia. He's tried to have her broker's license pulled. He had her investigated for stalking.

"He managed to get a restraining order that keeps her from blocking his gate, but she just stands to the side and takes her photos whenever she wants. The thing is, she hasn't published or said anything about him publicly, at least not yet. Now, whether she knows anything about this cruise I can't say. More to the point, she might not tell you even if she does."

"What Roy is trying to say is that Lydia isn't good at sharing," said Murphy. "Among other things, she's bipolar. When she's particularly agitated, she has the vocabulary of a sailor. I don't see the point of bringing her into a Key West matter. She's not a local. She'll just drive people crazy."

"The thing is," said Roy grinning, "she likes Murphy. For a while, he liked her too, until he figured out she was only boinking him to get information for her documentaries."

"That's bullshit," said Murphy.

"Maybe that's more information than we need," I said. "I don't see the harm in just telling her what we know and asking if she'd like to help."

"Then what?" asked Murphy. "Let's assume Lydia had a passenger list for the cruise. What are you planning on doing with it? You can't just call these people and ask them whether they saw a girl being murdered. You won't get past their media people. Most likely, you'll hear from their lawyers. In the best outcome, you'll reduce the passenger list to a few likely suspects, but how would you determine who might have seen something? Anyone on that cruise pays dearly to be kept out of controversy, and any whiff about murder will send them into max protection mode. Plus, Giles's lawyers will be all over you the moment one of the passengers complains. Your legal bills will be astronomical, even assuming you could find someone to represent you."

When I didn't respond, Roy gave me a knowing look. "Sucks, doesn't it?" he said. "I know how it feels when money counts more than the truth, but that's how the world works."

"Okay, we're back to where we started," I said. "Megan's killer goes free and Giles can do whatever he wants with Alicia. If there's another girl — someone on that boat who might know where Alicia is, and Lydia knows how to contact her — then I'm willing to put up with one more crazy person if it means keeping Alicia alive and getting a shot at Giles."

The four of us sat quietly, digesting our lunch and the harsh realities offered by Detective Murphy. I watched Roy, the muscles in his face twitching, his eyes unfocused. "Makes sense to me," he said finally. "I'll call her."

Detective Murphy rolled his eyes. "So, we're back to talking to Lydia."

"Can't hurt," offered Tess.

Detective Murphy scowled at her. "Might not hurt you, but I want no part of that woman."

The subject matter exhausted, Detective Murphy and Roy fell into a joint lecture about how the criminal justice system is imperfect, how guilty people go free, and how innocent people are convicted. He pointed out that when money or power is involved, the system works differently. Giles Horan simply had too many friends and knew too many secrets. His money, his friends, and his secrets made him untouchable. These explanations for why Giles always managed to dodge prosecution were familiar, and I had grown indifferent to them.

Looking back, I should have paid more attention. According to Detective Murphy, justice for someone who claims to be above the law is still possible, *only it looks different*. He insisted that if you're claiming to be above the law, *you can't hide behind the law to protect yourself.* To the extent that I considered it, the conclusion seemed like a platitude, a statement of principle without consequence. A more cerebral review of Detective Murphy's words and the way he said them would have revealed the statement as a justification for acts previously committed and for those that might be performed sometime in the future.

*****

After Detective Murphy and Roy left, Tess and I sat on the pier, looking out at the blue water. Birds of all sizes skimmed the surface, doing what they had done for thousands of years. They ignored us or, more precisely, took no notice.

Tess turned to speak. "Here we are, in this beautiful place, surrounded by water and birds and sunshine. Hard to believe we spent our afternoon with two aging, bitter cops discussing why a young girl was dead and another was running for her life. I'm not sitting here communing with nature, thinking spiritual thoughts. No. I'm angry at a man and worried about a girl, neither of whom I'll ever meet. If that weren't enough, I know I will need to deal with Hank at some point but dread the moment when he calls and begs me to return. I don't know what I'm going to do with the rest of my life, but based on what I've accomplished so far, I worry that I'm just going to hop from fixing one mistake to another. Most people sitting here would be embracing some Oprah wisdom about enjoying the moment, but if I try to jam one more thought into my brain, my head will explode."

"I think you have bright future, assuming Giles doesn't kill us."

Tess gave me a puzzled look and then burst out laughing. "Are you trying to comfort me? That's really messed up. Funny as hell but messed up." She buried her head in her hands. "How did we get here?"

I moved my chair closer to hers and watched as an egret soared by. "Birds live according to a plan that nature has devised for them. I had a plan before coming back to Key West. I hadn't looked too far down the road, but I had found a career I was passionate about. I was offered my dream job — tracking fish populations *and* playing with statistical software. I know that combination doesn't tickle most people, but it made me giddy. Then Ethy had a stroke and that plan, such that it was, had to be tossed aside.

"I came to Key West thinking I would stay with her until she recovered sufficiently to care for herself. Then that plan proved unworkable. Plan three, which encompassed renovating my mother's house and having you take care of Ethy, was just too simple to crater, and yet, with my chance encounter with a dead girl's body, even that plan had to be put on hold."

Tess smirked at me. "A smart person would consider giving up planning. I think I will. Life just gets in the way, and you're back to where you started, or worse."

"Before you said that, I was going to suggest that we focus on finding Alicia and getting our hands on the laptop she stole. We make nice with Giles. He leaves town. Maybe I'll teach you to dive and count lionfish."

"Is that plan number four? It sounds easy."

It did. But, of course, it wasn't.

CHAPTER TWELVE

By the time we left the restaurant, it was late afternoon and time to check in on Ethy. Before we arrived at the house, my phone rang. It was Clara Morse.

"I would have called you earlier, but I got no use for a phone when I'm not at home. If you want to talk to Rachael about Alicia, you need to be at my house. Don't go to the church 'cause Pastor Simmons is there and for some reason he don't like you and 'cause I seen some folks hanging around there that don't belong in this neighborhood. Could be just tourists wandering around, but I don't like seeing strangers with nothin' to do but look at you and take pictures of your house. You hear me? Anyways, come to my back door, and I'll let you in. Should be dark by then."

Ethy's insistence that she "not be left alone all day and all night in a big house" proved quite the buzz kill, and she wasn't mollified by my promise to call her as soon as the meeting was over. Tess announced that she had a headache and needed to lie down. Ethy took the opportunity to blame me for making Tess miserable.

"I don't know what you said to that girl, but you need to make it better."

I shook my head. "I haven't a clue what —"

"I heard her crying last night. She was on the phone and telling you she was sorry, that you needed to understand how you'd put her in a difficult position. I mean, I didn't hear all of it, but if by —"

"Listen. Listen. She wasn't talking to me. She was talking to her fiancé in New York."

Ethy stared at me. "Fiancé? No one told me she even had a boyfriend."

"I learned about him this morning. Please do me a favor and don't say anything to her about this."

"You're not dating?"

"I have to go. I'll be back later."

*****

Even with the grand parade days away, traffic entering town was frustratingly slow. I parked at my house just as the sun sank below the horizon and set off for Clara's house, hoping Rachael would be more inclined to trust me with Clara there to vouch for me. I entertained the thought of a kumbaya moment, after which she would lead me to Alicia, I would retrieve the laptop, and...The fantasy ended, not just because it was beyond stupid, but because it raised one big question I couldn't yet answer: What would I do with the laptop if I retrieved it?

The fading light left the tree-lined streets blanketed in a translucent shadow, a fickle hue that drew some streetlights out of hibernation while others slept. The patchy lighting created ominous zones of darkness perfect for street thugs and other miscreants to hide. I chided myself for letting Giles and André make me paranoid but quickened my pace nonetheless.

Using the light app on my phone, I navigated to Clara's back door. I was about to knock when the door flew open and I was

116

ordered inside. Clara led me to a small sitting room where Rachael was pacing. Without looking at me, she stopped and said: "If you've got something to say, say it."

I talked through what I knew about Megan and her relationship with Alicia. When I recited what André had told me, Rachael dropped into a chair and buried her head in her hands. She looked up, her glistening eyes reminding me of the mess I'd made of things. A moment later, she did so verbally.

"For the love of God, you have no idea what you're dealing with. You've got a heart full of good intentions and a head filled with images of homeless girls pining for home. They aren't. By the time they get here, they're feral. They're throwaways. No one's looking for them because they aren't wanted. The ones who make it here have acquired survival skills the hard way. A few make it back to the world you live in. Most don't.

"I understand that what happened to Megan is a tragedy and what is likely to happen to Alicia is regrettable. But nothing you do will make it better for her. Nothing. Still, you keep sticking your nose into other people's business, and now we got men hanging around, watching what we're doing, thinking we're hiding something. The girls I'm still caring for don't feel safe. You've got to stop."

"I need to find Alicia and the laptop she stole. Once Giles gets back what he wants, he'll leave you alone."

Rachael shook her head. "You're not listening. She isn't going to give you anything. If she stole something really valuable, she's not trading it for some promise by a hired thug or a well-meaning stranger. She wants to be independent, to fly away like a bird escaping a cage. All she talked about was how she was going to hit it big one day and help Megan and a girl at the shelter named Kizzy have a normal life." Rachael groaned softly. "Good lord, that child

117

doesn't know what normal is. In her mind, the laptop is a ticket out. You have nothing to offer her to make her want to give that up."

"Who is Kizzy?" I asked.

"Kizzy's barely thirteen. She's an emotional wreck, most of the time living in a world inside her head. How she got here is a story that would break your heart. But when Alicia showed up in town, Kizzy was a different child. Alicia would walk her to school and fill her head with dreams of being a happy family. Last week, Kizzy told me how she would be leaving soon, how Alicia was going to get them a new life, how they were going to buy a house somewhere and start over. It was bizarre. Alicia is seventeen and smart, but she isn't capable of taking care of herself, much less someone like Kizzy. But Alicia doesn't see it that way. She dreams of having money, and lots of it. She'll never give that up."

"Then she'll die," said Clara. "Giles will find her and kill her."

Rachael shrugged. "I know, and I accept that. All I can do is offer these girls shelter. I can't change how they see the world because their view has enabled them to survive. You have to understand that. You have to understand that you can't reason with a child who only believes what she can see or touch. Your assurances and promises don't matter squat."

"Would Alicia try to contact Kizzy?" I asked.

Rachael rubbed her temples and looked doubtful. "Maybe. Kizzy was listening to a message on my answering machine the other day and ran away when I confronted her. That was the day before yesterday. I listened to it, but no one was speaking — it was just noise, like someone had butt-dialed from a crowded room. I heard what sounded like the word *mud* a few times. It made no sense to me, but it seemed to make Kizzy happy."

"I'd like to talk to Kizzy," I said.

118

Rachael shook her head. "She's too fragile."

"I'm the best chance Alicia has of coming out of this situation alive," I said. "I just want to see if she knows where Alicia is."

"I think you should let Jake talk to her," said Clara. "What's there to lose?"

Rachael glared at me. "Kizzy's in the living room playing with Clara's cats. Before you go charging in, understand that she's fearful of men and has reason to be. She may see you and run. Even if she stays, she may just withdraw, and once she's back in her shell, you won't get her out." I turned away, but Rachael stepped in front of me. "Any sign you've upset her, and you'll leave her be. Understood?"

I nodded, asked Clara for a length of yarn, and approached the living room dangling it as bait.

The living room was a small space made more so by an odd collection of furniture, cat trees, and scratching posts. Kizzy was sitting in the middle of the floor, the object of attention of three kittens vying for ownership of her head and shoulders. The yarn attracted the attention of an orange tabby cat who chased and batted at it enthusiastically.

I sat on the floor a few feet from Kizzy and cast the yarn in her direction. "I call this cat fishing," I said. "You want to try it?"

For a moment, Kizzy ignored me. Then she grabbed the end of the string and pulled it toward her. The three kittens and the tabby gave chase. She smiled as they took turns pouncing on it, falling over, and chasing it again.

"Do the kitties have names?" I asked.

Kizzy looked at me, making eye contact for only a moment. She pointed at a gray-striped kitten. "That's Daniel. I had a brother named Daniel. The black kitten is Licorice. Daniel was always eating it. It made his tongue black. The girl kitten is a calico cat. I don't have a name for her yet. The orange kitty is Trouble. That's his name because he's always climbing the curtains or pushing things off counters. He may be my favorite."

"Did Alicia like to play with cats?"

A scowl flashed across Kizzy's face. She scrambled to her feet. "I want to leave."

Rachael appeared and took her hand. "Let's go, honey. You've had a long day."

"Does the word *mud* mean anything to you?"

Kizzy ran to the front door. "Leave me alone. Leave Alicia alone." The door flew open and Kizzy ran into the night. Rachael shot me a scolding glare and then went after Kizzy.

Clara shut the door and picked up a mewing kitten. "I don't know what makes me sadder — seeing that child all tied up in knots or knowing that Alicia is playing a game she can't win."

Clara set the kitten on a cat tree, then looked at me. "I know what Rachael said is true, but so what? No kitten or child was saved by letting it struggle on its own. Sometimes it don't work out, but do nothing and it will end bad every time. I think you've done everything you can to make it right. You've got to quit now. These are bad people, and they'll hurt you if you threaten them."

She wrapped her arms around me and patted my back. "You're a good boy. I know you're trying to do the right thing. The right thing now is to go home and be with your girlfriend."

I stepped from Clara's house into a heavy mist. The streetlights were mere islands of soft light hovering above dark pavement. It was easy to imagine being the only inhabitant of a world made of fog, that I might wander in this cloud of gray forever and never find my way back home. But while I could muse about being lost and alone, I knew I would never grasp the reality of it, that I would never know the hardships that life had thrown at children like Megan, Kizzy, and Alicia.

My phone rang and I knew without looking at it that it was Tess wanting to know what I'd learned about Alicia. If I were to answer the question honestly, I would acknowledge that her situation was hopeless, that Alicia's fate was out of our hands, and that we needed to accept it. I answered the phone certain that honesty wasn't what Tess wanted.

"Hey there," I said. "I was about to call you. I met Rachael…"

"Jake, stop. It's Murphy. He came by to talk to you and collapsed. He's been taken to Fisherman's Community Hospital."

"Is he —"

"We don't know. Just get here as soon as you can. I've got to go too."

The news about Murphy left me distracted, so much so that I failed, at first, to notice a silver Mercedes emerging from the fog and pulling right in front of me, blocking my path. The driver exited the car and stood behind an open door. As best I could determine in the faint light and mist, he was a tall man of about fifty with the build of a linebacker. His right hand was tucked inside a light-colored sport jacket, a pose that was both a cliché and effective. He told me to keep my hands where he could see them, which struck me as silly given I had no place to hide them.

A moment later, the passenger door opened and a man in a suit stepped out. He came toward me, instinctively buttoning the middle button of his jacket. He was a few feet from me when he said, "Good evening, Mr. Savage. My name is Giles Horan. The man beside the car is Bruno. He's not going to hurt you unless you give him cause."

He paused as if waiting for an indication of deference. None was offered.

"Not exactly your part of town," I said.

"You're a cocky one, I'll give you that. But you're way out of your league." He extended his hand in the car. A moment later a young girl slid out the door and stood beside him. "This is Beth. Say hi to the nice man."

Beth was dress in a short skirt and T-shirt. She smiled but didn't speak.

"I'm sure you're telling yourself that I'm a disgusting sexual predator, but deep inside your dick is whispering a different story. You lie to yourself. Me? I'm more honest than you and I have far more money. So do my friends, the people who were on my yacht."

I looked at my watch. "Is there a point you're trying to make?"

Giles shoved Beth back into the car and set his jaw. "I'm fucking trying to do you a favor, Mr. Savage, so show me the courtesy of listening. Megan was on my boat. The last time I saw her, she was alive. There were fifty people on that cruise, good people with charitable instincts and noble causes. If one of them made a mistake, if one of them killed Megan, so what? Megan was street trash. Even her parents didn't want her. I strongly suggest you let me handle this and you go on looking at fish and grieving over your white trash mother."

I took a step toward Giles which prompted Bruno to stiffen.

"One more thing. I've got people around me that I can't trust. I'm sure you've met André. Tedious but nasty man. Not someone you should listen to."

122

Giles tossed a business card onto the road, then slipped into the back seat of the car. A moment later, the Mercedes was gone.

I stared into the mist that seemed to swallow the street. Earlier in the day I'd been threatened by André. Now I'd received a threat from Giles. The chances of pleasing either or both of them seemed increasingly remote. I glanced at the card lying on the wet pavement.

"Fuck both of you," I said, and walked away.

*****

I don't like hospitals. I've actually never stayed in one, but I spent a lot of time hanging out in this particular facility waiting for my adopted father to die. If it were just the association with his death, I think I could get over it. But the smell, the sounds of people expressing their emotions or trying not to, the faces of people who have reason to hope and those who don't — all of this stirs my instinct to flee. Such an instinct is exhausting when ignored.

The door to Detective Murphy's room was open. I peered in and saw Ethy and Tess next to the bed of a man they barely knew. When I stepped inside and Detective Murphy looked at me, he rolled his eyes and shook his head. "Jesus, you'd think I was your rich uncle or something."

"Roy said you had money," I replied. "Just one more lie in a world full of fake news."

"I'm not here by choice," said Ethy, giving Tess a blameful glance. "I was ordered to get into her car in a voice that I thought was unacceptably harsh."

Detective Murphy pointed to the door. "Do I need to spell it out for you? You should all leave. I'm not dying — okay, I am, but not imminently. I just fainted because the chemo gave me the trots and I was dehydrated. It's not a big deal. Please. Just go home."

"What brought you to Ethy's house?" I asked.

"I found one of Lydia's flyers asking girls involved with Giles Horan to come forward. Her phone number was written on removable tabs at the bottom of the flyer. About half the tabs — maybe twenty — were gone. I wasn't keen on you talking to Lydia, but then it occurred to me that she might have heard something from Megan or Alicia. I gave the flyer to Tess."

A nurse arrived and told us if we were going to agitate her patient, we would have to leave. Outside the room, I asked her when Detective Murphy would be discharged. The question brought a look I'd seen before, an expression that conveyed both sympathy and bad news.

"I can't discuss his medical condition except with family."

"What if he doesn't have any nearby? The people in that room cared enough to come here. I know there are rules, but I don't see anyone else coming to claim him as a husband or a brother, do you?"

"We've told him he needs to check in at an assisted living facility that offers hospice care. The facility we recommended is quite nice and the people there will make him as comfortable as possible. But he just curses and pretends he's not dying. Maybe you can talk some sense into him. But if he's stable, he'll be able to leave tomorrow morning. I know he's in pain, but he refuses a morphine drip. I'd give him a week before the pain becomes unbearable. Keep an eye on him because when it happens, it will happen quickly."

I thanked her, then joined Tess and Ethy in the lobby. I conveyed what the nurse had told me, which didn't seem to surprise them.

Tess handed me a slip of paper. "This is Lydia's number. I was going to call her before Murphy went all wobbly. You were going tell me about your visit with Rachael and Clara."

"I'll spare you the part where Rachael ripped me a new one. The takeaway is that no one has heard from Alicia or has any idea where she might be. Alicia may have called another girl named Kizzy, but Kizzy wasn't interested in talking about it. Rachael insists that looking for Alicia would do more harm than good. The highlight of the evening was Giles insisting that he wasn't involved in Megan's death."

Tess gave me a puzzled look. "You spoke to Giles?"

"He stopped me outside of Clara's house for a nice chat while his driver, Bruno, made sure I didn't kill him."

Ethy turned and looked down the hallway in the direction of Detective Murphy's room. "Sad to think a man like Detective Murphy is dying when a skunk like Giles keeps on breathing."

Tess took Ethy's arm. "I'm sorry I barked at you. Let's get you home."

Ethy pulled free. "I'm not crippled." She glared at us, then walked away.

I left Tess with Ethy and headed back to Key West, unwilling to revisit the events of the day or to consider what anything meant. I called Lydia a few times and left messages, but halfway home, I tossed the phone on the passenger seat and turned on the radio.

I crawled into bed and stared at the ceiling. I'd shown a complete stranger a photo of two girls standing near a yacht, and I'd paid big time for that mistake. Any thought I could move on from André and Giles, that I could forget Megan and Alicia, that tomorrow I would return to a normal life, was complete fiction.

I wasn't initiating events but reacting to them, like a dead body carried by a current to an unspecified location.

As I lay on my mattress listening to the mice scurrying in the attic, I wondered how it would all end.

DAY 5

THURSDAY, OCTOBER 22

CHAPTER THIRTEEN

I was up before sunrise following a night full of dreams and nightmares. The most memorable was loosely based on an experience when I was sixteen. I was working on a salvage boat off Cozumel, Mexico when we spotted a cabin cruiser that looked to be in distress. No one was at the helm, and the hatch door was open. We hailed them on the radio and, when no one answered, launched a rubber zodiac raft to see what was up. I went along for the ride because I had a knack for working on engines and electrical systems.

The buzzing of the flies should have been a warning, but I went straight down the hatch to the sleeping quarters to see who was on board. Just before the smell hit me, I saw dark stains on the walls and ceiling. Four bodies — those of a man, a woman, and two children, each with a single slash across the throat, their faces covered with flies — were stretched out on the floor. I was only there for a moment before one of my mates pulled me up the stairs and back to the dingy, but the images have haunted me ever since.

The captain of the salvage boat reported the boat to the Mexican authorities and were told to leave the area immediately. I never found out who the victims were or why they were killed, but from time to time they visit me at night, and I talk to them.

Last night in my sleep, I traveled back to the boat, drawn by a familiar voice to the cabin where the bodies were lying. Inside, I found my mother sitting next to a young girl who looked like Megan. While I couldn't remember the details of last night's conversation, I awoke blanketed by an unshakable gloom.

After two cups of strong coffee, my mood improved, assisted by an email from ClearSeas announcing a new lionfish survey area near the Dry Tortugas. The email suggested better times, which was amusing in itself given that I had only encountered the body of Megan Jones a few days earlier. Those "better" times didn't seem so terrific while I lived them.

I sent Don Clayborne an email requesting more information about the Dry Tortugas survey as a pretext for asking him to use his contacts to find out what he could about André Mitchel. I wasn't sure what I'd do with the information but asking couldn't hurt.

I worked on my house. I made money servicing boats. I spent time on the water. I kept an eye on Ethy. Often, I complained about how tedious life was, how unsatisfying the renovation was, how poor I was. Now I longed for the days before Megan cast her shadow over me, when I controlled my life, when I could decide how a day would unfold, when I had to clean gobs of drywall dust from my nose and pull splinters from my hands.

I read the email attachments several times while imagining days on the water and nights on board, logging data, drinking beer, and eating freshly speared fish. As appealing as those images were, I knew escape was not an option. For now, I was a player in a real-life drama in which my life and the lives of Alicia, Giles, and André were connected, the actions of one directly affecting the other. The drama would soon play out to its end, whatever that would be. My future, it seemed, was in the hands of people I didn't really know or had never met.

I was pulled from this line of thought by the sound of two trucks pulling into my driveway. Instinctively, I looked inside my house for a weapon. The best I could come up with was a short pry bar, a decent implement to attack a stubborn nail but sadly insufficient against a trained assailant with a knife or a gun.

I peered out the front window and was relieved to see José Perez, a skilled contractor who had done some of the heavy work on my house, coming to the door. I opened the screen and ushered him in, his broad toothy smile spread across a tanned and weathered face.

"Mr. Jake, good to see you. I hope you are well."

"I am," I said, "but I'm confused. I don't think we had anything scheduled for today."

José shrugged. "Some people scheduled work, then cancel at the last minute. This isn't good for business. My crew comes from Miami, and now they are here and can't work. I can't pay them for not working."

He shrugged again, leaving it to me to work out his intention. José was a clever negotiator. I had learned not to let him lead me into a trap, which meant letting him negotiate with himself.

"That's true. Yet, here they are in my driveway. I don't see how that solves *your* problem."

Finally, José smiled. "You are a smart man, Mr. Jake, and for a homeowner your work is pretty good. But by the time you finish installing the electrical switches and outlets, sanding the drywall and painting, you'll be an old man with gray hair or even bald; and you need a new roof. Metal is good and goes up fast. I will install hurricane straps, make everything solid. You show insurance company pictures and they give you discount. Because we're friends, I will do that for what I pay my crew plus materials."

"The attic is full of junk and will need new insulation," I said. "But money is tight."

"How much you have?"

I laughed. "How much do you pay your crew?"

He pointed a finger at me and wagged it. "I like you, Mr. Jake, so I will paint the inside, finish hanging the doors and installing the baseboard, haul away all of your trash and replace your roof for two thousand plus materials — cash of course. Tomorrow I come back and sand your floors, make everything good. You will have a new house by tomorrow night. How does that sound?"

The last estimate I had gotten for just the painting and the roof work was nearly $4,000. Even so, paying José for labor and materials would consume most of what I had in savings.

We shook hands nonetheless.

"I suggest you take any valuables with you," he said. "I trust my guys, but why tempt someone? You need to pick up the paint while we're sanding. You will need two five-gallon cans of primer. You can pick a color for the final coat. If you are going to sell the house, paint all the rooms the same color, something light, because the new owner will paint it again." He laughed. "You can recommend me, and I will make up then what I lose today."

When I had started the renovation, I was convinced I could take my time. When I was finished, I would live in it whenever I wasn't on the water. Now, I was equally sure I just wanted to sell the place and move on.

"Some light color," I said. "Got it."

He shouted commands in Spanish and in a matter of minutes, the house was overrun by men with ladders, paint sprayers, and sanding blocks. I directed three men to the attic.

As José suggested, I gathered some clothes, my mother's letters, and a laptop computer and tossed them in a carry-on bag. I made a brief search for a small box of old Spanish coins I found while diving off a reef near Cuba, then realized if I couldn't find them, they were probably safe. I tossed the bag in the trunk of my car, then watched the three men climb into a truck. As they drove away, one of them pointed at the house and said the word "roof".

Excited by all this activity, I made coffee and heated a frozen breakfast in the microwave, taking pleasure in the sound of men at work and the thought that I would soon be relieved of a seemingly endless renovation. Denying the mice the run of my ceiling would also be a plus.

I was eating chewy pancakes when my phone rang.

"Good morning, Tess."

"Where are you? I can barely hear you."

"I can't hear you, either, but I'm headed to Home Depot to buy paint."

"Paint? What about paint?"

A compressor kicked on, filling the house with a low throbbing noise. I screamed into the phone. "I'm headed to Home Depot. I'll call you later."

In thirty minutes, I was pushing a cart through the paint aisles looking for primer. A well-meaning man with gray hair and bent fingers proceeded to explain the difference between paint and primer. "Good paint," he added, "has titanium dioxide pigments and costs a lot but covers better than paint with a lot of talc and clay."

What I thought was going to be a pick-up and run trip was turning into a complex cost-benefit analysis. I was saved when Tess appeared with an older woman whom I didn't recognize. The older woman looked at me and the salesman. "Men don't know shit about paint," the older woman said. Understandably, the salesman left. "What are you painting?" she asked.

"New drywall."

"How big is the house?"

"Not big. One story. A thousand square feet. Maybe fifteen hundred."

The woman grimaced. "That's the primer you need," she said, pointing to a five-gallon bucket. "Get two of those and keep the receipt. Now, for the final coat, you want to stay away from grays. That's passé. We'll get a nice off-white — a peach or earth tone — and that should do you fine. Once they mix it, you can't return it. Go with the peach. Very Key West."

"I don't think we've met," I said, offering the woman my hand.

"Not to my recollection," she said.

Tess did the honors. "Jake Savage, meet Lydia Carlson. Lydia heard about Detective Murphy from Roy Perching and came to see him. I met her at the hospital this morning. Jake's going to explain why we're buying paint, and then he's going to take us to brunch."

"He's buying paint because he's painting his house. Not a mystery. Let's get to the paint desk before they get too busy. They've got to mix it, and I'm starving. But before we fill our bellies, I want to see the house. I'm a real estate agent when I'm not sticking my nose in other people's business. Best to stop a man from making a mistake because it's impossible getting him to admit he made one."

I stopped at the bank on the way back to the house. Lydia used the time to express her feelings about Key West. "No one in their right mind would live here, but right-minded people are boring and stuffy. I don't like the traffic and parking's a bitch, but you can't beat the place for charm and weirdness. Of course, you need money. Even a dump in this town is worth a king's ransom."

My house is a small bungalow built in the late forties. Before succumbing to hurricanes, fires, and mansionization, the neighborhood had been full of these small dwellings

As we pulled into the driveway, I gave a short version of the deal I'd struck with José Perez.

"That's a lot of money," said Tess. "I mean, do you have it?"

Lydia sighed loudly and shook her head. "Money's not a problem, sweetie. When the work is done, Jake can refinance, take out the equity, and do quite well."

"Define *quite well*," I said.

"You own a home, but you don't watch the real estate market? So much education wasted on young people. I mean, sight unseen, your house is worth a half a million dollars, give or take. You can get a loan for eighty percent of that and pocket the rest. Use some of that for landscaping and exterior work and the rest to wait out in style your two years here."

"Two years?" I said sheepishly.

Lydia rolled her eyes. "Oh, dear. Live in it for two years and, when you sell, you get a capital gains deduction of two-fifty. Get married and that's five hundred thousand. Even if your basis is zero, you might get away tax free."

I looked at Tess. "Have I expressed my deepening feelings for you lately and the possibility of holy matrimony?"

"Your romantic overtures would feel more sincere if you were to send me flowers and a card promising a fifty-fifty split."

"Quick learners," said Lydia, sliding out the car.

José's crew took the paint, and Lydia followed them inside, leaving me to question Tess.

"Why did you bring Lydia here?"

"Well, I went to see Detective Murphy, and Lydia was visiting with him. Before I could leave, she insisted that I tell her what evidence we had that Giles was involved in the death of Megan Jones. As you can see, it's hard to say no to her. I told her about you, and she said something about getting crank calls from someone named Jake. Mostly, she asked questions but doesn't offer anything in return."

"Did she say why she was visiting Detective Murphy?"

"On the way here, she said she'd heard from Roy that Giles might be implicated in a murder. I guess he told her that Murphy was in the hospital, and she just showed up."

"Why did you go to see Murphy?"

Tess looked away. "My dad died in a hospital alone. I…I just did." A moment later, she flashed a smile. "How does it feel to be a man of means?"

Before I could think of a pithy rejoinder, Lydia and José appeared at the door of the house, chatting with him in Spanish. She returned to the car and motioned for us to follow. "Best to walk to the restaurant than circle the block looking for a place to park. I told José not to apply the top-coat until the primer had dried thoroughly. I know the owner of the Blue Heron. Brunch is good there, but don't order anything from last night's menu."

Lydia took off and Tess and I hurried to catch up. I wasn't sure how talking to Lydia would change anything.

But it did.

*****

Lydia disappeared into a Blue Heron restaurant packed with waiting diners. A few minutes later, she appeared, waving us past the line of grumbling, hungry tourists. We followed her into a small garden, where a table was in the process of being set.

"I convinced the owner to procure this property ten years ago. It didn't look like much then, but now it turns a good profit and employs a lot of people. This garden is usually private, but today it's ours to enjoy. I've ordered a fish dish I'm sure you'll like, which gives us time for you to tell me what you've learned about Giles Horan."

"I don't think so," I said firmly. "For all we know, you work for him or someone like him. I'd like you to first tell us who you are and why you care about what we know."

Lydia glared at me, her expression conveying anger and surprise that her demand had been rejected. A waiter arrived with three margaritas. Lydia drank half of hers, then leaned back in her chair.

"From what Trish has…"

"Tess," I said.

"Right. Tess has told me you're in a shitload of trouble. Giles is swinging his dick around like usual. I don't know this André guy, but he seems like a low-life from New Jersey. That's the bad news. The good news is that they don't know shit and think you might. For a while at least, that will keep you alive. But the clock is running."

"How about you tell us about how Giles ended up on your shit list," I said evenly.

Lydia drained her margarita and reached for mine. "I was checking listed houses in West Palm Beach when I found one

135

occupied by a group of teenaged girls. They were dirty, hungry, and frightened. If one of them hadn't been seriously ill, I'm sure they would have run off before I could talk to them."

"So what happened?" asked Tess.

"The short version is that I let them stay there, even had the water turned on, had a nurse friend of mine check on the girl with the fever, and brought them food. Over time, they told me about Giles Horan and what had happened to them. I convinced them to go to the police. That's where I met Roy Perching and Trent Murphy. The girls gave statements and it looked like Giles was going to go down for multiple counts of rape, sex trafficking, and kidnapping. But it didn't work out that way. The girls were publicly humiliated. One killed herself. The others disappeared into the streets. I let them down, made promises I couldn't keep. That was a few years ago. I backed off, gave up. One of the girls contacted me six months ago and thanked me for trying to help her. That's when I started watching him again. This time, I want to nail him."

"Roy said Giles leaves you alone but wouldn't or couldn't say why."

Lydia's face brightened. "I'm not going to tell you either." She leaned forward. "I'll just say that Giles hasn't been as careful as he should. Some of these under aged girls have babies. A little DNA testing and the father wouldn't be hard to find. I may have mentioned that to one of Giles' attorneys. I'm not saying any of these girls would come forward, but Giles doesn't know that. As long as I don't threaten him publicly, he's seems willing to let me take pictures and hang out at his gate."

Lydia took another sip from the margarita I thought was mine. "Cheap watered-down tequila mixed with sugar and lime and the tourists think they're in paradise. Margins on these things are ninety percent. Now you're going to tell me what I came to hear."

I explained how I'd found Megan's body, about tracking the tattoos, the maps showing the currents, and the conversations with André and Giles. "Giles says he wasn't involved. André says his client didn't kill Megan, but he seems to need the laptop to prove it. Assuming both are being truthful, one of the cruise passengers killed Megan."

I thought Lydia would accept the information as unhelpful and move on. Instead, the narrative I told seemed to excite her.

"It was Giles' yacht. Megan was under aged. Even if he wasn't directly involved in Megan's death, he can't afford that story to hit the news. He may not have killed her but hiring under aged girls to provide sexual favors to other men isn't legal. He's got a problem, and he's trying to solve it."

She pulled a phone from her pocket, fiddled with it for a moment, then showed me a photo of a group of people standing on a dock.

"I have a friend fly a drone over Giles' compound every so often. His charity cruise to Key West and Fantasy Fest was well publicized. He even arranged for his own drone, so when mine flew over, no one thought twice about it. We didn't get too close, but if you look to the right, there are four girls, including Megan and Alicia. You mentioned that the tattoo photo was taken by a young actress. On your left, at the front of the line, are Gwen and Dillon Farrell. Gwen isn't an actress, although she claims to be. Even so, the public loves her. Dillon makes a ton of money starring in action films playing the part of super stud Mitch Westly, which is good because his cocaine habit consumes most of his earnings. Everyone on the dock is waiting to board the *My Cloud*."

"If what you say is true, all these rich and powerful people are potential witnesses or suspects. I doubt any of them want to be connected publicly with the murder of a young girl. That's why Giles needs to shut this down. In the meantime, you need to find Alicia and that laptop she stole. Giles wants it. That André fella wants it enough to threaten you. Now I want it. We can get this son-of-a-bitch. I know we can."

"That's not going to be easy," said Tess. "No one knows where Alicia is or how to contact her. We're flying blind."

I retrieved my drink and drained it. "Not if Lydia can put us in touch with Gwen Farrell."

"I'll make a call or two, see what happens."

I was still trying to sort out my change in status from unemployed laborer to real estate mogul when I felt the gravitational pull of Lydia's agenda drawing Tess and me back into the search for Alicia and Megan's killer. Despite my misgivings, Lydia's enthusiasm was infectious, as was her desire to expose Giles for the scumbag he was.

The food arrived and the conversation ended. Lydia was an efficient eater, meaning she treated it like a task to be checked off a list. She was done and ordering coffee and dessert while Tess and I were still finishing our entrées. She drummed the table with her fingers and looked around the garden. "I need to mention something to you, and I don't want to freak you out. It's likely that I was followed to the hospital. I'd be shocked if I wasn't also followed to your house. Giles will know that we talked. He won't like it much, not after he told you to mind your own business. Same with this André fellow. If we're going to do something, we need to do it quickly, before either has a chance to exert leverage over you. They will search your lives for anything and everything you want kept secret. I'm sorry, but that's the way it works."

Coffee and dessert arrived. Lydia tossed three heaping spoons of sugar into her cup, tasted it, then added two more. "The message on Rachael's answering machine is puzzling. Can't imagine what the word *mud* means. Probably nothing. But you need to talk to her again and see if you can figure it out. I'm afraid you're going to have to squeeze these people to get them to talk, even if that means threatening them."

Tess and I managed a quick bite of dessert and a gulp of coffee before Lydia announced she needed to get back. She agreed to send me pictures of the passengers boarding the *My Cloud* and information she had about Gwen Farrell. As they left, Tess mouthed the words "call me," then scurried after Lydia.

Alone in the garden, I replayed in my head Lydia's entreaty to find the laptop. She had laid out a case for finding it, then made sure Tess and I were properly motivated by painting a dire picture of our situation vis-à-vis Giles and André. Her argument boiled down to, "You're probably going to die anyway, so you might as well keep looking for Alicia and the laptop." Lydia was all business — her business. We were pawns in a game she'd been playing with Giles for a long time. That made us useful but also expendable. She'd charged me with talking again to Rachael and deciphering the message left on her answering machine. But what was Lydia doing for us?

The question left me thinking about what Roy had said, about finding someone who had been on the cruise, someone in Giles' inner circle, who would be willing to chat. One name came to mind: Gwen Farrell. Unfortunately, the one person who might be able to connect us to Gwen was Lydia, but I didn't get the feeling Lydia was inclined to assist. I spent a few minutes imagining how I might contact Gwen myself before accepting that all the possible schemes would either get me shot or arrested as a stalker.

I asked for the check but was told it had been taken care of. I accepted an offer of more coffee and a young waitress returned with a decanter. "Stay as long as you like," she said. "I'll check back in a few minutes to see if you need anything else."

I futzed with my phone, reading again the message from ClearSeas about the lionfish survey, when I received a call from Don.

"You're in deep shit," he said.

"Okay. I get deep. Explain shit."

"Your friend André is the real deal. He kills people for a living, people who know something they shouldn't — witnesses, lowlifes who cut deals — and people like you too. There are rumors that he has cooperated with the Feds when it served his interest or the interest of one of his clients, but who knows."

"Not terribly informative, but worth knowing."

"Jesus, Jake. How did you step into this mess?"

"The question I really need to answer is how I'm going to get out of it."

CHAPTER FOURTEEN

On reaching Rachael's two-story Victorian house, I was still uncertain what to say to her. She again met me on the porch holding a broom like a weapon.

"You've got the persistence of a palmetto bug and about as much sense. Nothing's changed. I've got nothing to say to you."

"I'd like to hear the message left on your answering machine," I said, "and take a quick look at Kizzy's room. Then I'll leave you and not come back. Please."

"I know you think you're helping Alicia, but you don't know what trouble she's in or whether you're helping or making things worse."

Rachael propped the broom against the side of the house and motioned me inside. "No point looking at Kizzy's room 'cause the other girls tossed it a few times looking for whatever Alicia stole. They all want the reward. I suppose I can't blame them, but Kizzy's a mess. She didn't want to go to school today but going was for the best."

I stepped into a living room filled with bean-bag chairs, a sofa stacked with pillows, and a collection of cats sunning themselves on large windowsills. "The answering machine is on the sideboard.

You can listen to the message, but it's nothing but a lot of noise. Please do what needs doing and get out."

I scrolled through the message log until I found it — a three-day-old message. Curiously, the only call received on that date looked to be from an international number with the prefix 8816. I listened a few times, then recorded the audio on my cellphone. I had hoped to hear something in the message that others hadn't, but the message was as advertised. Two minutes of noise and a couple of audible words that sounded like "mud" but could have been something else. The message, it seemed, was useless. If the call was from Alicia, she had already left the country.

Rachael appeared, broom in hand. "Kizzy is due any minute. I don't want her to see you. Go and, for the love of God, please leave us alone."

*****

I was a block from the shelter when my phone rang. It was Don.

"You never said if the analysis I sent you was helpful or not. Any news on your dead body?"

"I'm sorry. The maps helped, but there's so much we don't know. I'll try to repay you somehow."

"Man, you sound like a guy who just lost his dog."

"It's complicated. I'm crosswise with some bad people. I'll leave it at that."

"Probably not the best time to bring this up, but we're filling out the crew for the lionfish survey. The plan is to focus on the small keys and shallow areas within twenty miles of the Dry Tortugas. I can get you on as a paid crew member, but you'll have to commit in the next day or two."

142

"I don't know. Two days feels like an eternity."

"Now you're worrying me. Talk to me…"

"I gotta go. We'll talk later."

It was nearly four when I returned to my house. The crews were packing up tools and trash. José met me at the door. "I wasn't sure you were coming," he said with a grin. "But then, I know where you live. Anyway, the walls are still wet. I'll come by tomorrow morning to touch up whatever we missed, do the floors, and check the traps we set in the attic. Just don't install the electrical outlet and switch cover plates for a few days." He handed me a stack of papers. "This is an invoice for the labor and what I paid for materials." He pointed to a number on the invoice. "That's what you owe me. You have cash?"

I pulled an envelope from my pocket and counted out the money I owed him. I had him sign the invoice as paid and thanked him.

"I can help you with the kitchen," he said. "Sometimes people buy a house and get rid of new appliances and cabinets. I can make you a good deal."

We shook hands and I stepped inside. What had been a construction site had morphed into a beautiful bungalow with light peach walls that seemed to glow in the afternoon light. I was still taking pictures of my beautiful new house when Tess called.

"Lydia's one weird lady," said Tess.

"A lady with an agenda. A lady determined to expose Giles Horan for who he is."

"She certainly doesn't much care about what might happen to us, other than we shouldn't die until she gets Giles' computer. So, what did you learn from listening to the voicemail?"

"Nothing. Looks like an international call to the wrong number."

The phone went silent.

"My house looks great," I said. "I'll send you pictures. I'm thinking about signing up for a lionfish survey cruise around the Dry Tortugas National Park at the beginning of November. You can come, too. I mean, what girl wouldn't be thrilled to be on a boat for ten days with a bunch of guys who like to drink, pass gas, and tell raunchy jokes? The corals and bird life are nice, too. You might get a glimpse of Fort Jefferson."

"Right now, that sounds pretty awesome. We'd need to find someone to take care of Ethy, but yeah. I could go for that. I haven't been to Fort Jefferson since I was in high school. I think we were studying the assassination of President Lincoln, but at the time I was studying a boy named Craig Something."

I heard Tess's voice, but I was no longer listening.

Finally, she said, "Are you there?"

"The message — the word 'mud.' What if it wasn't a reference to a thing but a person? Dr. Mudd was imprisoned at Fort Jefferson for his role in the assignation of the president. I think the call came from the Fort."

"But you said the call was from an international number. How would Alicia get access to a foreign registered cell phone? Even if she did, I don't think there's cell service that far out in the Gulf."

"Probably not, but when I was working on a treasure hunting vessel, the satellite calls from some carriers looked like international calls."

"I know you want the pieces to fit, but all you have are two audible words and a weird phone number. How would she get to the fort? Where would she stay? What would she do for food? And now you're saying she has a satellite phone? You're over thinking this. Watch some TV and go to bed. I'll bring Ethy by tomorrow and we'll inspect my house. Maybe we should have a party."

"Your house?"

"I thought about it, and I think we should get married. With a good divorce lawyer, I'm sure I could take my half and most of your half."

"They say you have trouble making commitments."

I grabbed a beer, then walked through the newly painted rooms. The paint had sealed the walls and they were no longer shedding drywall dust. Other than the smell of fresh paint, the house was already livable and evidently quite marketable. I would be financially set for the first time in my life. Against any measure, the day had been pretty awesome. So why wasn't I more excited?

The loose end that I couldn't ignore was the phone call. A federal park in the middle of the Gulf had to be able to communicate with the mainland. The obvious solution was either a land-line or a satellite phone. But how would Alicia have gotten access to either? More to the point, how would Alicia have gotten to the Fort without being identified? To find out, I couldn't go back to Rachael, but I could talk to Clara Morse.

*****

Clara wasn't home, so I took a seat on her front porch and waited. She arrived a half hour later pulling a small cart full of groceries.

"I don't see you for like twenty years and now it feels like you're moving in," she said. "Make yourself useful and take these groceries inside while I get my aching feet out of these shoes."

145

I followed her inside and was immediately swarmed by hungry cats. The challenge was to get to the kitchen without stepping on or tripping over one.

"I'm sure you got something to say, but before you get to it, I need to feed these guys and get myself a nice bourbon on the rocks. I can make you one if you like, but I won't be social until I'm on my second."

I declined the drink and passed the time playing with the kitties that Kizzy had entertained the night before. Clara watched, occasionally making odd guttural sounds.

"I watched you do that when you was just a little boy. You and cats have a thing. I'm surprised you don't have one."

"Wouldn't be fair to have a cat if you're not home to keep it company."

"True enough." Clara swirled her glass, then let out a sigh. "You go ahead and tell me why you're here."

"I needed to ask you if Alicia said anything about going to the Dry Tortugas, to Fort Jefferson."

Clara swirled the bourbon in her glass, then drained it. "I didn't speak much to her, mind you. If I did, she wouldn't have told me where she was going. But now that you mention it, I saw her with Karen Pasqual last week. Karen has a small shed in her yard that I think Alicia was sleeping in. Karen is an odd duck even by Key West standards. Gets a bit uppity about the strangest things. Tried to tell me once that my flowers were on her property, then got mad when I moved them. But then she collects stray cats. I take care of them when she's gone."

"Would Alicia tell Karen where she was going?"

Clara shrugged. "I didn't hear what they was saying. But

what you're missing is that Karen works at the park and is there now. I haven't seen Alicia either. Could be coincidence but makes you wonder."

I was writing a story in my head — a story about a girl hooking up with an odd woman who collects strays, a woman who worked on an island a hundred miles away where no one would look for someone like Alicia.

"Has Karen ever called you from the park?"

"Once, when we was expecting a storm, she called to ask me to check her house."

"Do you know if she used a satellite phone?"

"I don't know one phone from another. My recollection is that the connection wasn't good. We kept talking over each other." Clara leaned forward and pointed a finger at me. "You think Alicia is at the fort?"

I nodded. "The word *mud* could mean Dr. Mudd, the surgeon who set John Wilkes Booth's leg. The call to Rachael's answering machine wasn't from a domestic phone. You saw Alicia talking to Karen-- someone who works at the fort. It fits. Maybe because I want it to."

Clara filled her glass. "Karen takes the ferry to the fort. All Alicia had to do was to put on baggy clothes and she'd look like all the other bored kids being dragged around by her parents."

She sat next to me and patted my hand. "Now you got to decide what you're going to do about it."

I looked at her and shrugged. "She's safe there."

Clara stood up. "For how long?"

"I guess I could go to the fort, grab her, and drag her to the ferry without being noticed."

Clara ignored my attempt at humor. "Wait here." She left the room, returning a moment later with an Amazon box. "Karen orders things from Amazon and has them sent here. I take it to the ferry, and they deliver it to her. This came yesterday. If you show up with an Amazon package and ask for her, no one's going to think anything of it. Tell Karen what you know, and maybe she'll try and convince Alicia to trust you."

I took the box, realizing this might be my ticket to finding Alicia.

*****

A few blocks from my house, I heard sirens. Then I smelled smoke. Firetrucks, their lights flashing, lined the street in front of my house. A crowd had gathered behind a police line, the people drawn to the flames like moths to a streetlamp.

I ran toward the fire, only to be stopped by a policewoman. The flames streamed from the front windows; defying geysers of water poured on them from multiple locations. A skylight suddenly exploded as sparks and fire burst through. A loud crack was followed by the collapse of part of the roof. I watched silently as the last connection to my biological mother surrendered to the beast that devoured it.

"That's my house," I said frantically.

"I'm sorry, sir, but it's not safe to get any closer. If you wait here, I'll see if the fire marshal has time to talk to you."

"Fire is an amazing force," said a man standing next to me. "We can't live without it, and yet it's not ours to command — not completely anyway. But this fire is the kind we fear. A house, a place where people live. This fire is all-consuming. Angry. A home destroyed by an angry fire is a horrific thing, but yet we can't help but watch. It's ugly and beautiful at the same time. All of these men, with all their hoses and axes and hoses, can't stop it. The best they can do is make sure it doesn't spread to the other houses nearby."

A flicker of orange light revealed André's face.

I dropped the box and grabbed him by the throat. "You did this!"

He pushed my hand away. "I don't like being touched, much less grabbed or yelled at. See to it that you don't do it again. I said you were asking too many questions, but you wouldn't listen. This is what happens when you fuck people who have power. Stop whining and accept that you're in deep shit."

A window shattered, sending shards of glass into the yard. André seemed mesmerized. "Just when you think you've got the world in your hand, it's taken away. Control, you see, is an illusion. I met an interesting young woman — a girl with red hair and a funny name. Kizzy. Who would handicap a child with such a name? She was walking home from school and I was on a bench holding a kitten. Kizzy, as you know, loves kitties. Not me. They are arrogant, calculating creatures that keep too many secrets to my way of thinking. But Kizzy wanted to hold him. I told her I had a litter of kittens that needed someone to take care of them, that I would pay her if she would do that. She came home with me to see them. I gave her a snack and she fell asleep. Things can happen to children who are trusting, just like things happen to houses. I know you've talked to Giles. I'm certain he's threatened you. I want the laptop, and there's only one. That puts you in a bind. You have to trust one of us."

"I don't have the fucking laptop and I don't know where Alicia is! I can't help you!"

André groaned. "Now that isn't the positive attitude I expected from you. I'm sure you want to help Kizzy."

"You'd hurt a child to get what you want?"

"I do what I have to do to fulfill my client's needs."

"Fuck you."

André sighed loudly. "Crassness is beneath you. My client asked me to clean up a mess involving his son. If my client gets the laptop, he has the power to protect you and those you love from Giles. He can protect Alicia. Sadly, Kizzy will be left to her miserable life in some dismal shelter. There are limits to what even he can do. On the other hand, if you give Giles the laptop, he will make your life hell. He hates to lose. You might think you can outsmart him. You can't, but I can. I'm your best option. The sooner you get that through your head, the better off you'll be."

"Are you really asking me to trust the man who just set fire to my house? Just saying it out loud makes me feel stupid."

André laughed. "When you say it that way, it does sound a tad far-fetched. Even so, because you are naïve and wanting to do the right thing, you find yourself leaning toward the unlikely. That attitude is precisely how you got into this mess. Maybe you thought that finding out what happened to Megan would bring you some kind of peace. Then you thought you should save Alicia. These weren't rational choices, but just things damaged people do. Now you're trying to find a rational solution to the mess you made by being irrational. Actually, it would be amusing if it weren't so tragic, but such is human nature."

I shook my head. *Damaged people*. I hadn't thought of myself in those terms, but maybe it was fitting.

"While I find conversation with you stimulating," André continued, "we both know you don't stand a chance against Giles, me, or anyone of our ilk. We both know that this situation is going to end badly. For whom is all that remains to be determined." He handed me a card. "When you realize that you're fucked, call me on that number. Oh, I trust you have insurance. You might actually come out ahead. No need to thank me."

André walked away. I retrieved the box Clara had given me and watched as the fire hoses were shifted to my car, a clear indication that the house was now an official lost cause.

Just a few minutes earlier, I had been celebrating a small victory. I had a plan to find Alicia. I had a renovated house worth a lot of money. I was going with Tess to survey colonies of lionfish. For a brief moment, I was in control of my life, a fallacy quickly exposed by Giles and André and the flames that had reduced my house to rubble.

The policewoman returned and led me to the fire marshal. He was a tall man with a graying beard. He began speaking without an introduction or any pleasantries, explaining that the speed of the fire suggested arson, but that a final determination would only be made after a thorough investigation. Arson, he emphasized, was a serious crime most often committed by someone who would gain financially from the destruction of the property. Bottom line: I was not only the victim, but also the prime suspect. I was waiting for a Miranda warning when Tess, Ethy, and Murphy appeared from the crowd.

"Murphy brought us," said Tess. "I'm so sorry. What's with the box?"

"I'll explain later." I turned to Murphy. "What are you doing out of the hospital?"

"I don't like stewed beets and the nurse giving me a sponge bath wasn't my type. More to the point, the chemo seems to have given me a stay of execution. I actually feel rotten, which is a big improvement."

151

Murphy looked at the house, then at the fire marshal. "Jake didn't do it," he told him. "Stop looking for the easy answer and go find someone who plays with fire."

The marshal said something disparaging and left. For a moment, the three of us gazed at the small bungalow now completely engulfed in flames. Murphy broke the silence. "I think we should talk."

CHAPTER FIFTEEN

We climbed into Detective Murphy's car and, with lights flashing, rode to Castro's Last Stand. He spoke to a waiter and in a few minutes, we were seated at a table at the back of the veranda. A propane heater was moved closer to Ethy. She insisted she wasn't cold, but the heater was lit despite her protests.

"I'm going to tell you how things are," said Murphy. "Nothing will bring back Megan, and Alicia is long gone. If the fire had been set when Jake was sleeping, you all would be planning a funeral. Give it up."

"It's good advice, but it's a bit late," I said. "André won't stop at burning down my house. He's kidnapped Kizzy. He says he'll hurt her. I doubt it, but I can't take that chance. If I get him the laptop, he'll let her go."

"How do you propose to do that?" asked Detective Murphy.

"The call on Rachael's answer machine came from a satellite phone. Clara told me that her neighbor, a woman named Karen Pasqual, who works at Fort Jefferson, was helping Alicia. That's where I think Alicia is hiding. I'm going to take the ferry tomorrow to see if Alicia is there. I'll talk to Karen and hopefully to Alicia."

"That's it?" asked Tess.

The news was greeted with cold stares.

"Giles and André are playing with you," said Murphy. "You're a soccer ball and they're just kicking you from one end of the field to the other. One of them is going to finish you. What you need to do is to leave Key West and take Ethel and Tess with you."

"I'm not going anywhere," snapped Ethy.

I turned to Ethy. "No, you're not."

Looking at Detective Murphy, I said, "If we run away, then what happens to Kizzy and Alicia? I know it's a long shot, but what does doing nothing accomplish?"

"I'm confused," said Ethy. "Whatever you're saying sounds dangerous."

"I agree with Ethel," said Tess.

"What if André hurts Kizzy and I do nothing to try and save her?" I looked at Ethy. "You think I'm mental now? You think I could live with that worm squirming in my head? I can't fight Giles or André. I just need to convince Alicia to give up the computer. After that, André and Giles can fight it out between themselves."

"Then I'm going with you," said Tess.

I stared at her, conveying with my eyes what I couldn't say out loud. "You need to take care of Ethy."

For a few minutes, the only sounds were Ethy's sobs and occasional sighs from Tess.

I turned to Detective Murphy. "Take them home. I'm going to finish this."

I squeezed Ethy's hand, then left the table.

By the time I returned to my house, the last of the flames had been extinguished. All that remained was a charred concrete foundation filled with smoldering rubble. An hour later, the fire trucks departed.

My car, fortunately, had escaped serious damage. Some of the paint on the side closest to the house had blistered, but that would be invisible to the untrained eye. I opened the back door, tossed in the Amazon box Clara had given me, and put my head down, vaguely aware that I had just joined the ranks of the homeless.

DAY 6

FRIDAY, OCTOBER 23

CHAPTER SIXTEEN

I awoke to find a rooster on the hood of my car, strutting back and forth, impatient for daybreak. When I closed my eyes, the rooster crowed, pulling me out of my slumber. I slid out of the car, then took the opportunity to extinguish a smoldering piece of wood by relieving myself of last night's coffee.

Despite the rooster's announcement of the new day, daybreak was still an hour away. From my phone, I logged on to the Dry Tortugas National Park website and tried to book a ticket. As I feared, my card was maxed out. I used Ethy's card number and was rewarded with a "success" message and an e-ticket. I was reminded that boarding began at seven.

I had an hour to get to the ferry terminal. Before leaving, I retrieved a wrinkled and stained hooded sweatshirt and sandals from the trunk of my car. I'm sure I looked, and probably smelled, like a man who'd slept on a park bench, a man whom most people would intentionally ignore.

Normally, the walk to the terminal would take twenty minutes, but after doubling back and watching shadows for would-be stalkers, I arrived with only fifteen minutes to spare.

The sky began to lighten just as the boarding process began. Tourists carrying towels and snorkeling gear were already standing in line, apparently eager to get breakfast and to claim table space in the inside cabins. I stood back, keeping my face down, and watched for signs I'd been followed or was being watched.

Finally, I joined the stragglers and climbed on to the Yankee Clipper III. Managing to first snag a bagel and a cup of coffee, I headed to the upper deck. As the boat pulled away from the dock, a young woman in a similar outfit came toward me. She lifted her head and smiled.

I caught a glimpse of our reflection in the glass windows that enclosed the cabin. We might have passed for two refugees from a street cult hatching a nefarious plan to take over the boat.

Then Tess pulled back her hood and took a bite from my bagel.

"You didn't really think you were going to go without me?"

I did, but I was happy not to be.

"Now, look to the stern, at that man wearing a hooded shirt and holding a cane."

"You're kidding?"

The man turned and waved his cane at me.

"Shouldn't Detective Murphy be in bed?"

"He said he could sleep on the ferry as well as anywhere. He wants us to ignore him, so stop staring at him." She gave me a critical look. "Nice outfit, by the way. What's with the box? You seem to be attached to it."

I held it up. "This is our ticket to finding Alicia."

*****

Tess and I were on the upper deck when off to the northwest, the outline of the Fort appeared on the horizon. Mirage like, it

158

appeared to be floating, its towers and structures rising out of the water with no visible means of support.

The fort claimed a piece of history when Dr. Mudd, convicted in the conspiracy to assassinate Lincoln, was imprisoned at the fort. The brick structure and the surrounding reefs and keys had been incorporated into the national park system in 1992 and had, over the years, become a popular destination for tourists.

The ferry deposited its human cargo on a dock at the front of the fort. Access to the interior is via a bridge that spans a moat. Once across the bridge, we stepped through an archway and into a cavernous foyer. I approached a man dressed in a crumpled light gray shirt with two breast pockets and dark green cargo pants. Above the left pocket was a gold badge. Above the right pocket was a metal name badge with the name "Nick Francis" etched in black letters.

"Good morning, Nick," I said. "I have a package for Karen Pasqual. I was wondering how I might contact her."

He looked at the box, then at me. "You friends with her?" The question conveyed more than a little surprise.

"I'm friends with her neighbor back in Key West, so kind of."

A sly smile spread across Nick's face. "That makes sense. If you and Karen were friends, you'd be about the only one she's got. Wait here."

Ten minutes passed, and I began to doubt that Karen had taken the bait. Tess took to reading historical placards and pamphlets and sharing factoids.

"Did you know that the fort has six sides and was built using sixteen million bricks? The eight-foot thick walls encircle a large parade ground, which is accessible through open archways. But... the fort was never finished because newer cannon technology could blast through the walls. After the civil war, the fort was used as prison, and was home to several of the Lincoln conspirators, including Dr. Samuel Mudd."

"Very interesting."

"I'm sure you didn't know this. Metal doors that cover the gun emplacements were designed to fly open when the guns were fired. Before you think that was clever, consider that the iron mounted on the brick rusted and expanded, causing the bricks around the gun doors to fall out and almost causing the fort to collapse."

"No good deed goes unpunished."

I was spared another history lesson by the appearance of a tall, silver-haired woman coming toward me. She took long, fast steps and her arms swung wildly. As she came closer, her down-turned mouth signaled she wasn't happy to see us.

"What in God's name compelled you to drag that box all the way out here? I'm just going to have to take it back to Key West, which is of course where I wanted it left."

"I'm sorry," I said, "Clara thought it was something you might want…"

"What in hell am I going to do with a garlic press in this godforsaken place," snapped Karen.

"No problem," said Tess. "We'll take it back. No harm done."

"You don't know that, Missy. What if it's broken? What if you broke it?" Karen stepped closer to Tess and looked down at her. "It's people like you that drive people like me to live in the middle of nowhere."

Karen snatched the box from my hands and turned to leave.

"I'd like to talk to Alicia," I said. "It's about her friend Megan, a young girl I found dead a week ago and a girl named Kizzy who's been abducted."

The face that moments ago conveyed annoyance now was filled with alarm and fear.

"I don't…"

"I get that you're rude," said Tess, "but don't insult us and yourself by pretending to be stupid. She's here. We need to speak with her. That's all."

"You were the one who found Megan?"

I nodded. "I want to know who killed her, and I want to save Kizzy if I can. Alicia's our only lead. You have my word that no matter what Alicia says, we won't expose her whereabouts."

Karen pressed the box to her chest. "If you found her, it's just a matter of time before others do. Crap." She looked at Tess then at me. "I don't know how she's going to react when she sees you… This way."

She turned and walked slowly down a corridor seemingly oblivious to running kids and adults reading maps. "The odd thing about Alicia and me," she said, "is that we both suffered because of our looks. I was an ugly duckling. Gangly, shapeless — all the things that make a woman unattractive. Alicia was punished because, at a young age, she acquired the attributes that men objectify. Older boys noticed and showered her with attention. Unfortunately, so did her stepfather.

"She fought with her mother about makeup, lipstick, and clothes. Alicia also complained to her mother about her step-dad. Her mom accused Alicia of flirting with him and making him angry. Then her mother saw her husband watching Alicia through a keyhole. That sent her mom over the edge. She took a lethal dose of pills and left her daughter full of guilt and at the mercy of a man she hated."

"Her mother killed herself?" asked Tess.

"She did. Her father told Alicia that her mom left a note saying that she didn't want to live with a daughter of weak morals. He told her that the only way she could be forgiven was to give herself to God and let him 'purify her.' That's what he called it. He got drunk and came for her. She left and never went back. She was fourteen and on her own. Now she's seventeen, running for her life, wild and quick to react. She trusts no one, not even me. I'm telling you this because even if she talks to you, what she says is just as likely to be a calculated lie as it is the truth."

"Will it matter that Kizzy's life is in danger?" I asked.

"How the hell should I know?!" Karen's voice reverberated in the long hallway. "Sorry. I don't know what makes Alicia tick or what she values. She's very private, even with me."

"Caring about someone like Alicia has to be tough," said Tess.

Karen nodded. "I collect strays. I used to limit myself to cats and dogs. Apparently, I've branched into helping abused girls." Karen emitted a short laugh. "Pretty much the same skill set."

We came to a set of stairs that led to the second floor. A sign announced that the area ahead was restricted to "authorized personnel."

"The stairs are part of Bastion D." We both stared at her uncertainly, and she rolled her eyes. "Always stuns me how people can come here without ever reading what we post on the Internet. A bastion is a projecting part of a fortification built at an angle to the line of a wall that allows defensive fire in several directions. We have six walls and where they intersect, there's a bastion.

"Anyway, the staff lives in gun rooms between Bastion D and Bastion F that have been converted into apartments, each with a kitchen, living room, and bathroom. Some of the employees stay even when their shift ends, but every ten days or so, I go back to Key West to care for my animals. Clara watches them while I'm gone. I'm thinking about helping out Rachael at the shelter after I get back the next time. As I'm sure you've noticed, I'm not much of a social animal, but the animals accept me for who I am and are grateful for any help I provide."

Karen was in motion again, speed-walking through the narrow corridor closest to the fort's interior. We arrived at another set of stairs. "When the tourists show up, Alicia takes refuge in Bastion E. Most of the time, she listens to music, but sometimes, in the early evening, she sings. I'm certain that the staff has heard her, but no one seems to care. To be honest, it's pretty, almost ghostly to hear her songs reverberating through these old walls."

The stairs spiraled upward, depositing us in the small corridor on the second floor. A young woman was sitting in one of the small archways, her eyes closed, small white wires tracing a path from her ears to her cell phone. As we stepped toward her, she sprang to her feet, her eyes focused on us, calculating, building a profile based on a life of dealing with strangers. What I didn't see was fear.

If I didn't know her age, I would have been hard pressed to guess it. Long locks of hair cascaded over her shoulders, framing an angular face marked by high cheekbones and a pointed chin. Her lips were full and slightly turned down, conveying a sultry pout that seemed natural. But it was her eyes that captivated me. Cold and piercing, hers were the eyes of a cat patiently deciding whether I was threat or prey.

I pointed to her earbuds and she pulled them out of her ears. "Giles and a man named André want the laptop you stole. André kidnapped Kizzy and burned down my house. Giles made threats that were less specific."

"Why would they send you?"

"No one sent me. I found Megan floating in the Gulf. But it seems like I asked too many questions about Megan and you. That's why I've been threatened. André has threatened to hurt Kizzy. We thought you should know. We need your help to save Kizzy."

Alicia brushed off her shorts and casually flipped her long hair off her shoulders. "Well, now I know." She reached for her earbuds and pushed one into each ear, then walked away.

Tess started after her, but Karen grabbed her arm.

"What? You thought she'd see you as heroes coming to save her? *You* see a girl who ran away from home who can be saved with hugs and sweet words. Alicia didn't just run away, she was discarded. People like you saw her on the street and looked the other way." Karen pointed a finger at my face. "Men like him looked at her and thought of ways of pleasuring themselves. But here you are, with a story about needing her help and you think Alicia's going to listen to you?"

Karen turned and headed down the steps. "We're done here. Walk around. Go snorkeling. Go home."

I caught up with her at the bottom of the bastion. "You've got a lot of attitude but very little common sense. We aren't just two young do-gooders. We are a preview of what's coming. If we found her, Giles will find her, and he's not the only one looking. If you care about Alicia as much as you put on, you'll know that we're the best of her bad options. Talk to her. Get her to come with us."

"You've done what you came to do. Go home," she said, and disappeared into the endless expanse of red brick archways.

Tess and I headed back to the front of the Fort. At Bastion D, she grabbed my arm. "I know this is too late and won't make any difference, but I'm sorry how this turned out. I encouraged you when I shouldn't have."

I ran a finger over her cheek. "Here's the thing. We don't *know* how this is going to turn out. I don't know what Giles and André are going to do to you, Ethy, me, or Alicia, or what will happen to Kizzy. The worst of it is that I can't stop them. I'm sorry, but Alicia was my last hope. I'm out of ideas. But I don't blame you for any of it. Hell, this is the way we are. No point fighting it. But when we get back, you and Ethy are going to have to find a safe place for a while. That sucks, but we're out of options."

It was just after eleven. The ferry departed at three. Four hours with nothing to do but to count the sixteen million bricks and try not to think about the future.

Tess and I strolled around the fort and read historical markers about powder magazines, cisterns, and officers' quarters, none of which I remembered five minutes later.

Tess stood in the middle of the parade ground and twirled slowly. "Can you imagine spending years cooped up in this place? I mean, it's beautiful for a day, but dealing with the bugs and the lack of water and the heat, not to mention the smell?"

"Almost as bad as being married."

Tess gave me a stern look that slowly softened into a smirk. She laughed, then hit my shoulder. "You can be an asshole sometimes." I tried unsuccessfully to suppress a chuckle which prompted another blow to my arm. "Stop. It wasn't that funny."

A moment later and still snickering, she pressed her head to my chest. "What am I going to do?"

I took her hand and we walked back to the ferry and ate lunch. I looked for Detective Murphy, but he wasn't occupying any of the deck chairs on the stern of the top sun deck.

A little after one, Tess and I took a walk on the beach. The blue water that surrounded the fort was calm and inviting. Just yesterday, it seemed realistic to contemplate joining a survey ship to count lionfish in these waters. Now, I had no idea what tomorrow would bring. I was stuck in a limbo that seemed endless, waiting for events to make decisions about what I would and could do and when.

I spotted Karen coming toward me carrying the Amazon box. The realization that the fate of this package was a priority while the future of a young girl was left to the whim of a sexual predator both amused and saddened me. For a moment, I toyed with the parallels of an unwanted box and an unwanted child, only to chide myself for trivializing the latter.

She handed me the package. "Alicia wants to speak to you about going back with you. I think she wants to save her friend, but who knows what she's thinking? Take this thing back to Clara."

Karen spun around and headed back to the fort. Tess and I followed, quickening our gaits to avoid being left behind. When we arrived at the entrance to Bastion E, Karen stopped and faced us. "One thing I forgot to mention. One of the staff said he thought someone — a man — was watching us. The man was stopped before he could enter the fort's residential area." Karen shrugged. "The area is marked with a big sign that says it's for authorized personnel, and yet people just ignore it every day. It's probably nothing."

Unfortunately, it wasn't.

CHAPTER SEVENTEEN

Alicia was sitting on the floor, holding a small duffel bag. That she was packed buoyed my spirits. That all of her earthly possessions would fit in a single carry-on bag reflected how difficult her life had become.

If she noticed us, she pretended not to. Indifference, it seemed, was an act of aggression, an affirmative statement of independence that conveyed she was not coming with us because we asked her to but because she chose to.

"I'll let the three of you work things out," Karen said. She disappeared down one of the long hallways, her heel clacks echoing against the bare brick walls until she came to a stop.

I stepped toward Alicia, eager to commence a negotiation that could save Alicia, Kizzy, and me. She stood, her eyes focused on mine, determined to establish herself as an equal, as a force to be dealt with.

I spoke first. "If you have something to say, say it. We don't have much time."

"You can't let anything happen to Kizzy because of me. I'll tell you where it is, but you have to promise."

I shook my head. "You know better than us that we can't promise an outcome we don't control. All we can do is our best."

Alicia glared at me. "Pardon me if your best doesn't inspire confidence."

She held a plastic bottle of water, her eyes focused on the label. "I love Giles. People like you won't understand that, but despite what he's done, I owe him. He saved me from my stepfather. He taught me how to survive. But I also hate him for what he did to me and Megan and the other girls. I hate him for what he made me do. I hate myself for who I am. He made me this way, but I let him."

"But you didn't leave him?"

Anger flashed across her face. "I'm so tired of that fucking question…" She took a breath, closed her eyes, then re-opened them. "No one leaves Giles without his permission. To get that, you have to recruit your replacement. I recruited Megan. She was thirteen. I was promised a bonus for that, but Giles had his attorney explain that by recruiting another girl, I was participating in sex trafficking. He made me promise to keep quiet about that, but he also said that no one would believe me anyway. Stay quiet and you get what Giles called an allowance. It's not enough to live on, but you can't live without it. He still owns you, even after you're gone. Anyone who leaves without obeying the rules is punished. He'll publish photos, tell lies, spread the shit you've done all over social media. I've asked to leave lots of times, but all he says is that I'm not ready. In the meantime, Megan was getting deeper into drugs and other things…"

"Tell us about Megan," said Tess.

"I brought her in and did what I could to make things easier for her, to protect her. She clung to me like her big sister. I guess I liked that. She was more into drugs than me. She spent a lot of her money on cocaine, something that Giles didn't give us for free. Having a drug habit made her more loyal to Giles, so he was good with it as long as she did what customers liked. Lately, she'd been getting really fucked up and her clients were complaining. Giles wasn't happy with her, but Dillion liked her — Dillon Farrell, the actor."

"How did you try to protect her?" I asked.

"The best gig was a cruise on Giles' yacht. We were given great clothes and jewelry. The food was good, and the passengers were less icky. Giles would assign us to a male passenger who came without his wife. We would stay overnight with the passenger at a resort in Key West harbor. Usually, you'd get a good tip and there was always something to steal. Giles didn't seem to mind much if the thefts were small and not from him."

I started to ask another question when she put up her hands. "I need to tell you what happened."

"Sorry," I said. "Please."

"Dillon Farrell and Peter Cobb took Megan to the lower deck, where there are guest bedrooms. Dillon had a thing for her. Giles keeps cash and drugs in his office, which is on the middle deck toward the front of the boat just before you get to the master suite. With Giles talking to his friends on the sun deck, I thought I'd see if I could get past security and into his office. I flirted with some men at the bar, but most everyone was outside. I took one of the canvas bags they gave out as souvenirs and slipped out of the bar. I was surprised how easy it was. I went to Giles' office and started rifling his desk.

"That's when all hell broke loose. Security guys came running and shouting. I slipped into a closet, which was full of electronic equipment. On a monitor, I could see one of the guest bedrooms where a small crowd had gathered. Several men were hovering over the bed. Someone was in it, but I couldn't see who. Dillon was standing to one side, naked. Peter was partially clothed, lying on a couch. I couldn't make much sense of it. I looked for Megan but didn't see her."

"This is all after Megan was killed?" asked Tess.

"I think so. I guessed Megan could have been on that bed, but I couldn't see her face. I had no idea that something had happened to her. Everyone was talking at once, but I couldn't tell what they were saying. Then someone came into the office, and I dropped to the floor. That's when and where I saw the laptop. Whoever it was left. I disconnected the computer, slipped it into the bag, and opened the door. The lights flickered and then went off completely. I ran out and reached the bar when the lights came back on. Something about a generator problem. I stowed the bag and waited until we docked."

"Did you hear anything about what had happened below?" I asked.

"No, but Gwen was a mess. She doesn't usually drink much, but she was tossing down shots and crying. Anyway, my escort helped me with my bag, and we got off. He's a nice old guy. I've stayed with him before. That night, to his surprise, his wife was waiting on the dock at the resort. I thanked him for his help and left him to sort things out with her. I was waiting for the shuttle to Old Town when he found me, slipped me $500, and told me how much he appreciated my discretion. I didn't tell him how much I appreciated his Rolex, which I'd stolen before accepting his money. I hid the laptop. When I realized that Megan was dead, it was too late to go north, so I came here. That's it."

I looked at Tess. "I'm guessing the laptop was being used to capture video from the bedroom," I said. "If that's true, it's evidence of Megan's murder."

"Lovely story."

We turned and saw Bruno standing at the entrance to the bastion, his hand pressed across Karen's mouth and a gun pressed to her head. Both were shoeless, explaining their stealthy arrival.

I stepped forward, only to be commanded to stay where I was. "This is what we are going to do," he said. "Alicia is coming with me on a seaplane and will give me the laptop. The three of you will stay here until someone finds you. In this heat, it won't take long."

He released his grip on Karen, then shoved her toward us.

He pointed his gun at Alicia. "I believe my young friend was about to tell me where she hid the laptop." He screwed a silencer onto the gun barrel. "I'm waiting."

"Screw you, Bruno," said Alicia, defiant.

"Come on, sweetie," replied Bruno. "After all we've been through together, there's no cause to be ugly. You're smart enough to know when you're on the losing end."

"Not sure how killing the one person who knows where the laptop is will endear you to your boss," I said.

"Actually, I'm not working for Giles at the moment. Think movie star with a lot of money. Bonus points for retrieving the laptop, but as you said, Alicia is the only one who knows where it is. So, without her, it will remain lost. I still get paid. Kind of a win-win. Easy money for sure." He waved the gun. "What will it be?" When she didn't answer, he extended his arm and aimed at her head. "I'm going to have to insist that you answer my question."

The bastion was located at the intersection of two walls that were part of the ring forming the six-sided fort structure. In each wall segment, an inner corridor opened to the parade ground.

A larger corridor opened to the cannon installations and faced the sea. Where Bruno stood was close to where the inner and outer corridors of these two walls met. Locating the source of a distracting noise at this confluence is difficult.

We all heard what sounded like a piece of wood hitting the walkway close by, but from where? Bruno stepped back and turned his head to the left. He guessed wrong. From his right, a man wearing a hooded shirt rushed at him and swung what looked like a cane down onto the gun, separating it from Bruno's hand.

Bruno turned his huge frame and, with his powerful hands, grabbed his assailant by the throat. What looked like a certain death grip lasted only a moment. The hooded man brought his right shoe down on Bruno's bare left foot. A scream of agony filled the chamber as Bruno fell to his knees, followed by a sickeningly hollow sound of a cane hitting the back of his head. I chased down the gun while Tess held Alicia. Karen, frozen in her tracks stared blankly at the two men.

Bruno's attacker fell forward, then rolled over, revealing the face of Detective Murphy. I ran to him and helped him up. "What the hell are you doing?"

He groaned. "Saving your ass," he said. He glanced at Bruno. "Is he dead?"

"No."

"Shame," he said, looking at the gun in my hand and then directly into my eyes.

I slipped the gun in the waistband of my jeans.

"Are you hurt? Shouldn't you be on the boat resting?"

"I'm not spending my last hours sitting in a chair drooling on myself," Murphy said. "Besides, other than a sore neck, I'm having fun." He leaned over the unconscious Bruno, removed two seaplane tickets from his pants pocket, and handed them to me. "Get Alicia out of here."

I shook my head. "What if Giles is waiting at the airport?" I said. "You and Tess take the flight. I'll go back with Alicia." The detective scowled. "You know I'm right," I added. "Meet me at the ferry terminal. We'll get off last."

I turned to the others. "We need to leave now, before he wakes up."

"Security won't find him here for a few hours," said Karen. "I doubt he'll want to confess to trying to kill us, so more than likely he'll make up some bullshit story about slipping on the steps. The boat is full, but the captain agreed to let Alicia travel back with you."

Alicia and Tess helped Detective Murphy down the stairs to the lower level. Karen took me aside. "I know Alicia said she would help you, but don't deceive yourself into thinking she trusts you and, for God's sake, don't trust her. It's not her fault, but she will lie about anything to get what she wants. Right now, for her, that passes for control. Mind you, she's never had it, but she is always trying to acquire it." I started to leave, but she grabbed my arm. "I feel as if I owe you an apology. I might have misjudged you. I have no idea why you and your friends would want to protect a girl like Alicia, but thank you."

*****

The seaplane boarded on the beach on the fort's east side. Alicia stood with Detective Murphy while Tess and I stood at the back, watching the stream of passengers to determine if any of them were watching us.

Tess glanced at me a few times but remained silent. "If I were a gambling man," I said, "I'd bet you were fighting the urge to tell me something. The longer you wait to spit it out, the more I'm inclined to think it's bad news."

"I spoke with Hank last night. He wants to come here and work things out." Tess pursed her lips. "I told him not to, that I was busy, and that we could talk later. Couldn't be worse timing. But I don't think he heard me. He's impulsive, so he could show up at any moment."

"Bad news has an agenda of its own."

Tess rolled her eyes. "Him just appearing is the last thing I need."

"How will he find you?"

"I told HR where to forward my last check. Hank knows a lot of people. I'm sure they gave him Ethel's address."

"What are you going to tell him?"

Tess shook her head, then walked away.

The seaplane pilot appeared and asked for tickets. A few minutes later, Tess and Detective Murphy got aboard the small plane. I watched as it taxied into the open water, then lifted off and headed skywards.

On the ferry, Alicia and I found seats at a table offering a clear view of the main cabin. We shared the table with an elderly couple, neither of whom seemed likely candidates to kill one or both of us. Alicia slipped in her earbuds and closed her eyes. A small woman with a cotton-white head of hair looked up from her book, smiled at us, then returned to reading. Her male companion, who was connected to an oxygen tank via a long length of clear plastic tubing, was busy working on a Sudoku puzzle.

At precisely three, the ferry pulled away from the dock. The fort was now in the hands of its caretakers, most of whom were relieved that another flock of ignorant tourists were on their way back to Key West. The structure and its sixteen million bricks slowly disappeared in a western sky while to the east and south towering thunderheads were turning the sky the color of a bruise. In thirty minutes, the boat was encased in the dark shadow of a looming storm while lightning flashed between the lowering clouds. A torrent of rain pounded the ferry from all sides. In the blur of wind and rain, flashes of blue-white light illuminated the cabin, causing some of the passengers to cower in fear.

Then it ended. Suddenly, the cabin was basking in bright sunlight. Many of the passengers ventured outside to enjoy the hues of pink and orange painted on the clouds that had so recently threatened them.

Alicia, who had remained calm during the storm, removed her earbuds and looked at me. "Do you think Bruno was going to shoot us? I've known him for years. He was always nice to me. I actually thought he liked me."

"If you mean you, rather than us, maybe not, at least not until he had the laptop. When he screwed the silencer into the barrel of his gun, I think the odds were that he wasn't going to leave any loose ends. The rest of us were fucked."

The lady across from me lifted her eyes from her book and gave me a scolding glance.

"Sorry," I said. "Just a few raw nerves from the storm. No offense intended."

"Nice to know someone's fucked," said the man with a laugh.

The woman hit him with her book, leaving the two of them giggling with amusement. "Can't take him anywhere."

175

Alicia started to re-insert her earbuds but hesitated.

"You didn't ask me where I hid the laptop."

"That's your decision. To be honest, I'm not sure what I'd do in your situation. Giles wants it back, but he's probably not going to pay you or forgive you. André makes promises, but then he burned down my house. I'm trying to save Kizzy, but you have to take my word for that. I'm not sure what good keeping it will do you, but you have to work that out for yourself."

The older man stared at his Sudoku puzzle, having stopped filling in boxes. "You live an interesting life," he said smiling at us, "not that I'm eavesdropping."

Alicia sighed loudly. "I taped the laptop to the bottom of a pew in the church."

She pressed the earbuds into her ears, closed her eyes, and turned the volume up. I heard the faint sound of gospel music and watched as she swayed to its rhythms, seemingly relieved of all her earthly burdens.

Assuming the laptop was where Alicia claimed it to be, the plan was simple. I would deliver the laptop to André. He would free Kizzy and use the power of his client, whoever that might be, to repel any attempts by Giles to retaliate against those involved in delivering the computer to André. All that was required to make this work was for André to keep his word.

CHAPTER EIGHTEEN

The ferry emptied slowly. Alicia and I waited with the stragglers and passengers with walkers to disembark. While she listened to music, I focused my attention on a half dozen men scattered about the terminal. They were pretending to loiter but were clearly watching us as we made our way to the exit. In unison, they converged on us, cutting off any chance of escape.

Alicia finally took notice. "What's going on?"

I handed her Karen's Amazon box, reached around to the back of my jeans, and found the grip of Bruno's gun. To be honest, the gesture was hollow, a moment of bravado before admitting defeat.

A bearded man wearing a T-shirt and cargo shorts came straight for me. A few feet away, he smiled broadly and showed me his ID. "You must be Jake. Detective Murphy asked that we escort you to his car, something about you and the lady here having information on a case he's working. Not sure what all the drama is about, but he's the detective. Anyway, if you follow me, we can get back to watching the streets."

Detective Murphy's car was parked on Grinnell Street. I was surprised to see him sitting in the back seat leaning against the door, his eyes closed. Tess was standing by the driver's door looking sad and exhausted.

"He insisted on coming, but I don't think he's doing well," she said. "I need to get him back to Ethel's house."

"What's wrong with him?" asked Alicia.

Tess glared at her. "He's dying."

Alicia joined Tess in the front seat, while I sat with the detective in the back. "So far so good," he said softly. "Let's get that laptop and call it a day."

The church was only a few blocks away, but traffic made the drive feel longer. As Tess pulled in front of the church, I leaned forward and removed one of Alicia's earbuds.

"This is the moment of truth. You can get out of this car, grab the computer, and disappear into the night. Or you can bring the laptop to me and let me make a deal with André. I don't have the energy to argue with you. Just do what you have to do, so we can get on with things."

Alicia slipped out the car, bypassed the front door and disappeared behind the building. A few minutes later, I saw her silhouette pass one of the large stained-glass windows decorating the sides of the church."

"I think she's gone," said Tess.

"Just wait," I replied. "We've come this far. A few more minutes won't matter."

The next five minutes seemed like an eternity. I heard Tess, under her breath, repeating the words "come on," and the more time that passed, the more my confidence waned.

The tension was broken by the sound of the passenger door

opening. "I couldn't get the last piece of tape loose from the bottom of the bench," said Alicia. "Sorry."

She returned to her seat holding a laptop crisscrossed with duct tape. For a moment, she held it, then turned and handed it to me.

I grasped it as if it were something sacred. In my hands was evidence of how Megan died, who was involved in her death, and who was involved in dumping her body into the Gulf. I imagined Giles sitting in a courtroom while the video was played before a jury, the arrogant, shit-eating-grin wiped from his face by evidence even his rich and powerful friends couldn't bury. I imagined it, but the fantasy was joyless. Giles would never face a jury for what he and his friends did to Megan, and the video on the laptop would never be introduced as evidence against anyone involved in her murder. In twenty-four hours, I would hand the computer to André. Kizzy would be safe, Megan's murderer would remain free, and the *My Cloud* would head back to Palm Beach. In the big scheme of things, Megan Jones never existed.

I asked Tess to drop Alicia and me off at my house, or what remained of it. It was still light enough to see the charred remains of what had been, a least for a few hours, a beautiful little bungalow. The scene of devastation seemed to transfix Alicia. Whatever she was thinking, she kept to herself.

A sign had been posted warning that the property had been condemned by order of the fire marshal. Another sign stated that the location was a crime scene accessible to authorized individuals only. I ducked under the police tape and brushed the ash from the windshield of my car. To my relief, the car started without bursting into flames.

I put the computer on the floor of the car, slid it under the driver's seat, then joined Alicia at what had once been my front door.

"I don't understand what's happening," she said. "I don't know who you are or why you're doing things. I just want to be free of him, of Giles. Now Megan is dead. Your house is gone, and a cop I don't know who saved my life is dying. None of it makes any sense." She kicked a piece of charred wood. "I didn't ask any of you to help me. This isn't my fault. It isn't."

*****

The trip to Raccoon Key was tedious. Because of the Festival, streets were closed, leaving drivers confused and angry. More than once I tried to make a U-turn, only to find the intersection blocked by police barriers and detour signs. Alicia sat quietly; lost in thoughts I couldn't begin to fathom.

When we arrived at the house, Ethy was enjoying attention from Tess, and Lydia was in a heated conversation with Detective Murphy. Alicia's entrance brought all that to a sudden end and cloaked the room in silence. A room full of smiling people eager to welcome her focused their eyes on her.

Perhaps it was the conversations with Rachael and Karen, but I found the empathy that filled the room was well intended but meaningless. More Alicias were being made each day; girls from broken homes and girls from homes with money were struggling with the problems that came with growing up, while their parents offered no solutions or simply made things worse. These were the children that men like Giles Horan preyed upon, and the supply seemed limitless.

The silence ended as words of welcome and comfort were offered. Lydia competed with Ethy for Alicia's attention. Alicia ignored them both. I grabbed a beer and headed outside, only to hear footsteps approaching from behind.

"Do you mind if I smoke?" asked Alicia, bringing a cigarette to her lips.

"I guess not."

Alicia shrugged. "What now?"

"How about I give you a talk about your future and you pretend to listen?"

The question was answered with a cloud of smoke blown in my direction. "Knock yourself out."

"Let's assume that Giles isn't in the picture. What would you do if you could do anything else?"

"You mean give up turning tricks and giving blow jobs to rich white guys? Let's see. I quit school in the ninth grade. I'm seventeen, soon to be eighteen. I can't see myself going to high school when I'm twenty. Can't go to college if I don't have a high school diploma. Why would I think about a future that I don't have?"

"Fair, but a bit defeatist. You can take courses online. You love music. I'm told you have a great voice. You could take piano or singing lessons."

"That takes money. I don't have any. Last I checked, you don't have any either, plus you're homeless."

"I'll figure something out."

Alicia inhaled deeply and blew out a cloud of smoke. Her silence made me wonder if she were imagining a different future, entertaining, albeit briefly, a hopeful thought about what could be. But if that was the case, the thought was quickly extinguished.

She tossed her cigarette on the ground and crushed it with her foot. "Right. I'm supposed to take advice from a guy who lives with his mother and doesn't have a job? Let's get something

181

straight. I don't need or want anything from you, and I don't owe you anything. What happened to your house isn't my fault. What happens to you and your friends isn't my problem. I'm not going to fuck you, suck you, or like you no matter what you do or say. All I need you to do is to save Kizzy. After that, I'll take care of her and myself." She took out another cigarette. "How about you give me some space?"

She walked away, leaving me with a bruised ego and feeling foolish.

I headed inside for another beer but, before reaching the kitchen, was stopped by Lydia. "You have the laptop," she said. "I'd like to see it."

"I don't think so," I said. "You turn that thing on, and God knows what might happen. Maybe nothing. Maybe it erases itself. I'm not taking that chance. Tomorrow, we get Kizzy back. André will deal with Giles; and, yeah, I know that whoever killed Megan gets a pass. That sucks, but —"

"But what? You get Kizzy back and Giles goes free? Is one girl worth letting that man stay out on the streets?"

"If it's on my conscience, yes, she is."

I left Lydia, grabbed a beer, and headed to the lanai. Tess was in a chair staring at her phone.

"Does the thought still count for something?" I asked.

"What?"

"Sorry. Just ...nothing. What's with the phone?"

"Hank. He keeps saying I'm his girl. I guess that's how men think, but it's really demeaning. I'm not a pet, or a slave, or a cow. He won't give up. Before he hung up, he said he'd see me soon, whatever that means."

I fell into a recliner, removed André's card from my wallet, and toyed with it, flipping it in my fingers, staring at it, then flipping it again.

"I know what you're thinking, but you have no choice," said Tess. "Even if Giles wins, we have to end this, for Kizzy's sake. The real problem you need to solve is how to protect Alicia from herself. She's got a lot of attitude and taking advice may not be one of her strong suits."

"How can you say that?"

I took out my cell phone and dialed the number on the card.

"I'm listening," André said.

"I have what you want. I'll make the trade for Kizzy, but I want assurances that Alicia will be protected. My only condition is that I want to see the video. I need to know what happened. I'm not sure if there's some security app on the computer. I need you to look at it, show me the video — somewhere public — and exit my life."

The line went dead.

Two minutes later, I received a text. "Truman House. Ten o'clock. One of yours sees the girl. One of ours takes the package out front. No cops."

"Okay," I said. "The show starts at ten tomorrow at the Truman House. I'm thinking that you and Rachael enter the grounds of the Truman House and look for Kizzy. I will make the swap out front once she's been secured. To keep things simple, Lydia and Ethy should take Alicia shopping. I don't want her anywhere near Kizzy when the exchange is made."

"Convincing Alicia to go shopping won't be easy," said Tess.

"Probably not. If all goes well though, Kizzy will be back at the shelter before lunch and we'll be back here."

"One more day," said Tess. "We get through tomorrow and we can start getting back to just being fucked up."

"You have a way with words," I said.

Ethy announced that food was available in the kitchen and that we all needed to eat it while it was hot. I thought I wasn't hungry until I saw a large platter of fried chicken, a bowl of fried onions and squash, and a basket of biscuits. As I filled a plate, I saw Lydia and Alicia in what seemed like a heated, but short, conversation.

With everyone served, Ethy joined Tess and me at the kitchen table. "Seems like everyone is enjoying themselves as much as can be expected under the circumstances," Ethy said, picking at a biscuit. "Sounds to me like Detective Murphy was a hero, although I don't know exactly what happened because no one will tell me."

"A man accosted us at the fort," said Tess. "The detective disarmed him. We escaped unharmed."

"Did the man die?"

I shook my head. "No one died."

Ethy stiffened, then stared at us. "But he works for that Giles fella?"

The question conveyed a judgment — that we had missed an opportunity to make the world a better place. It was a view that at least part of me shared.

"He did," I replied, "but I think Giles isn't going to be happy about what Bruno was up to."

Ethy seemed poised to ask a question when the doorbell chimed. She got up from the table.

"I don't want to discuss any of this," said Tess. "I'm just too tired."

Ethy returned and stood over Tess. "There is a tall man at the door in a dress shirt and wool slacks. He has lawyer written all over him. He said his name is Hank. I asked him to come in, but he said he'd prefer to wait outside. He said he was your fiancé."

"Damn it!" said Tess. She glanced at me, then at Ethy. "I've got to go."

Ethy patted her hand as she ran to the door. "I thought everything would get better when you found Alicia."

"So did I," she replied.

Lydia and I cleaned up the kitchen while Ethy made sure all the bathrooms had clean towels. Lydia elected to sleep in a chair in the room where Detective Murphy was resting. Before retiring for the evening, she took me aside. "First, I'm sorry for what I said earlier. I wasn't being fair. The other thing — after the exchange for Kizzy, I'd like you to help me get Murphy admitted to a hospice. I know he's determined to help you, but the man is pretty much dead on his feet."

I said I would.

Not long afterward, Alicia and Ethy headed to bed, leaving me alone in the living room nursing a pounding headache. I kicked off my sandals, stretched out on a couch, and closed my eyes.

*****

I heard the door latch click and sprang to my feet. Tess glanced at me but didn't stop. "I don't want to discuss this with you. Not tonight. Maybe never. I'm begging you not to ask me or try to help me. Let's get through tomorrow."

With Tess safe, I went to my car and retrieved my carry-on bag. I stretched out on the sofa and I read my mother's emails until I fell asleep to the sound of her voice telling me that everything would be all right.

DAY 7

SATURDAY, OCTOBER 24

CHAPTER NINETEEN

The room was still dark and, for a moment, I wasn't certain where I was. Then I awoke to the smell of coffee. Ethy appeared, handed me a cup, and hovered over me. "Now that you're homeless, I suppose you'll be moving back here."

For Ethy, these were caring words, conveying in an oblique way an invitation to come stay with her.

"Looks that way. At least for a while."

"I guess I'll have to get used to your ways again," she said, heading back to the kitchen. "It won't be easy. It never is with men around. You'll have to work for your keep."

"Probably a good time to mention that I used your credit card to buy a ticket to Fort Jefferson."

"You're starting to sound like my other kids."

Lydia emerged looking tired and gloomy. She took note of our questioning stares. "He's still alive, if that's what you're wanting to know. Actually, he got pissy when I offered him another dose of morphine. I don't know what's keeping him alive, but I think it has something to do with that girl Kizzy. He's demanded coffee and asked me to help him shower and shave."

Ethy chuckled. "If it's more than that, please don't tell us."

Tess appeared, avoided eye contact, and headed straight for the coffee pot. Even Ethy seemed to know better than to ask her about Hank. Coffee in hand, Tess went to the lanai, shutting the door behind her.

"If you're going to live here again," said Ethy, "you're going to have to learn to say what's on your mind without me trying to read it. You've been staring at those papers and then at me since you woke up. Either spill the beans or put them away."

I walked to the kitchen and laid the emails on the table. "I found these in the attic of my house. Did you know my father? Did you know anyone named James that she hung out with?"

Ethy wiped her hands, then sat down. As she read the emails, she stifled cries with the back of her hand.

"I didn't know his last name, but he was a handsome boy. He was smitten with Gretchen from the moment he saw her. A lot of men hit on your mother, but she didn't pay them any mind. James was polite and soft spoken. When she didn't feel well one night, he offered to drive her home. After that, he would walk her to work whenever he wasn't tied up at the base. I never understood what eventually happened to him, and your mom never let on."

Ethy sighed. "I suspect James' mother thought she was doing the right thing for him, but…So terribly sad."

"Do you know if she met with him when he came back?"

Ethy shook her head. "That was a long time ago. I seriously doubt it, but then she died just a few weeks after they were supposed to meet." She looked at me. "I can't imagine how meeting your father, if that's who he is, is connected to her murder."

I heard a door open and gathered the papers together. "Me neither," I said.

Breakfast was chaotic and almost comical. Ethy ran the kitchen, barking at anyone who offered to help. Her skill at running a bar was evident in her ability to produce food for five guests faster than it could be consumed. Tess joined Lydia, Detective Murphy, and me at the kitchen table for a feast of hash-browns, eggs, sausage, and toast. I explained the plan for swapping the computer, making it clear they shouldn't discuss the plan with Alicia until I called to confirm that Kizzy was safe.

Alicia appeared a half-hour later. Sans makeup, she actually looked like a teenager, even acted like one, too. Without wishing anyone good morning, she demanded to know when we were going to get Kizzy.

"That's up to the man who has her," I said. "Tess and I will go to town and wait for instructions. In the meantime, Lydia and Ethy have offered to take you shopping."

Predictably, getting Alicia to agree to a shopping excursion was a challenge that required numerous assurances that she could pick her own clothes and that if she wanted to return them, she could keep the money. The negotiations were peppered with questions about how we could trust André to keep his word. That prompted optimistic answers wrapped in caveats. Alicia remained skeptical but finally relented.

Tess and I were about to leave when Lydia approached me.

"Murphy wants to talk to you. He wants to come with you, but given the shape he's in, he'd be more hindrance than help. See if you can talk some sense into him."

Detective Murphy was lying in bed, his eyes closed, his mouth open. He seemed to be struggling to breathe. I turned to leave, but the sound of his voice stopped me at the door.

"I'm not dead yet," he said, "but I'll text you when I am. It's

189

the damned morphine. I can't keep my eyes open or my mouth closed." He patted the mattress. "Sit."

I sat on the edge of the bed.

"Hand me that glass," he said, "the one with the straw." He chuckled. "I came into this world wearing diapers and drinking from sippy cups. It looks like I'm going out the way I came in."

He closed his eyes and, for a moment, I thought he'd passed out. "I got a call from one of my friends at the office," he suddenly said. "You probably didn't know I had any, but I do. He tells me that this morning, they found a body in a dumpster near the ferry terminal. Apparently, someone called about the smell of rotting fish. From the description, it sounds like Bruno came back last night but did not receive the welcome he was expecting. That happens when you betray a man like Giles Horan. Keep that in mind. André is just like him. He's capable of anything."

"He must have made the fish smell really bad," I said.

"Probably." He closed his eyes. "Sorry. I'm tuning out. We'll talk later."

Tess and I left the house a little after nine. I managed to convince a policeman to let me enter old town in my car to meet an insurance adjuster at my house. The policeman was excited to relate his eyewitness account of the fire but in the end, he let us pass.

The so-called Little White House is located close to where Caroline Street meets Front Street. Like other towns that depend on tourists, Key West uses the names of famous residents to draw visitors and fleece them of money. While Hemingway is the most famous person associated with Key West — his house tops the list of "must see" attractions — Harry Truman and other presidents were also regular visitors to the island. The Little White House was originally built as housing for officers posted to the Key West naval base. The building was later repurposed as a single-family home and used by Truman multiple times during his presidency. Presidents are still free to visit, but its primary function is to entertain tourists as a Truman museum.

The lack of detail as to where we would find Kizzy left me wondering if we were walking into some kind of trap. For a moment, I wished Detective Murphy had come with us.

The sidewalk in front of the Truman House was clogged by people reading the historical marker and dithering over whether to pay the twenty-dollar entrance fee. Tess and Rachael made their way into the house while I stared at faces, hoping to detect some hint of recognition. To my surprise and relief, Tess called and announced that Kizzy had been spotted in the company of two men. Moments later, I was approached by a man with a map asking for directions to the Hemingway House. He directed me to a bench. Tess confirmed that Rachael was with Kizzy, but the men holding her hadn't left. I handed the laptop to the man with the map. He inserted a power-pack into the back of the computer and turned it on. He clicked a few keys, then handed the computer to me.

The video was surprisingly clear and disgusting. Dillon Farrell, the famous actor of action films, the man who as Mitch Westly had saved the country and the world from evil doers without concern for his own life, was violently assaulting a docile, probably drugged girl. He was behind her, towering over her, gripping her shoulders as he thrust himself back and forth. At one point, she screamed in pain and arched her back. Peter came into the frame and pleaded with Dillon to stop, but Dillon grabbed Megan's hair and pulled to keep her from escaping. Then Megan went limp and silent. Dillon continued until Peter pulled him off. Angered by the intervention, Dillon punched Peter, sending him out of the frame.

191

I saw enough to know who had killed Megan. I left the bench with the video still running. A moment later, Tess informed me that the men who had been with Kizzy left and that Kizzy appeared to be okay. The exchange had been completed.

I was waiting by the entrance to the Truman House when I felt a hand on my arm. "Don't turn around. Just listen." The voice belonged to André, but it lacked his usual bluster. "I kept my word — the computer for the girl. Just to set the record straight, I couldn't hurt a child. I want you to believe that. She's been sedated, but no one touched her."

André cleared his throat and for the first time seemed to struggle for words. "I'm a man of my word but my clients often are not. The man who paid me was Harold Cobb, the Attorney General of the United States. He promised me he would provide protection for all involved. I believed him, but now it appears that he's cut a deal with Giles. I'm not privy to the details, but the laptop will be given to Giles after all. As a consequence, Harold isn't going to protect Alicia or anyone else, leaving Giles free to be himself. He knows about you and your mother and your girlfriend. I'm afraid that Giles is going to mess with you because it pleases him. He's going to make Alicia's life miserable, probably by messing with Kizzy. Don't underestimate him. I'd tell you I was sorry, but it won't change anything. I regret setting fire to your house, but things like that happen. Take care, Mr. Savage."

I felt the hand leave my arm just as Tess and Rachael were exiting the house. The two women were all but carrying Kizzy.

"She's been drugged," said Tess. "God knows what they did to her."

Rachael slapped my face, drawing shocked looks from passersby. "You brought this on this child. You stupid, selfish man."

192

"That's not fair," replied Tess.

I looked at the small girl with the red hair, her eyes half open and fluttering, barely conscious. Whatever had driven me to delve into the death of Megan Jones and to find Alicia had blinded me to the collateral damage that my questions were causing. Having found Alicia and learned many of the details of Megan's last day on earth, I felt as if I'd accomplished nothing. Megan was still dead. Alicia would soon be hunted by Giles. Dillon Farrell was going to get away with rape and murder. My mother's murder was still unsolved. My house was ashes. Many memories of my mother had been forever lost.

"It's fair," I said. "Rachael is right. I'm sorry. Of course, being sorry doesn't change anything."

Rachael gave me a final scolding glance before disappearing into the stream of humanity on the sidewalk.

Tess tried to console me, but I wasn't interested.

"I've been a fool," I said. "Good intentions led me to make bad choices. I saw the video. Dillon Farrell killed Megan during a violent sex act. That wasn't the worst of it. André just told me that the laptop would be delivered to Harold Cobb, the Attorney General of the United States. While that might sound like a good thing, he's going to give it to Giles Horan as part of some deal I can't even begin to imagine. Giles is going to punish us, Alicia, Kizzy, and on and on. Excuse me if I don't take a victory lap."

I called Lydia and asked to speak to Alicia.

"Is she okay?"

"She's woozy from some medication. André didn't hurt her, if that's what you're asking."

"Who killed Megan?"

"Alicia…"

"Tell me!"

"Dillon Farrell. I don't think he meant to, but what he did to her was brutal.

There's something else you need to know."

I walked Alicia through what André told me about the deal between Harold Cobb and Giles Horan, but halfway through, she cut me off.

"I knew I couldn't trust you. I knew it. The computer is gone, and we got nothing for it."

"We do have Kizzy."

"I want to see her."

Despite my attempts to convince her it was dangerous, Alicia made it known that, with or without my help, she was going to see Kizzy. Lydia agreed to bring Alicia to the shelter and the call ended.

With time to kill, Tess and I found a coffee shop. To avoid conversation, we fiddled with our cellphones.

"Okay," she said, "I get why you're blaming yourself for everything that's happened in the last few days. André, your house, Kizzy — it's a shit storm for sure. But what about Megan? Didn't she deserve someone asking why and how she came to be floating in the Gulf? If you hadn't asked, no one would have. I'm sorry, but Giles wins because people let him, because he has leverage over the people who should hold him accountable. At least you tried to expose him. That should count for something."

"I suppose."

Tess touched my hand. "I need to tell you something."

"More good news?"

"I'm going back to New York with Hank. I can't explain why because I'm not sure myself. I suppose I owe him something better than just running away. I say I don't want to marry him, but what if that's just me being afraid? I don't think it is, but I can't hurt this sweet man until I am sure."

The chirp of my phone announced the arrival of a text message. "Alicia and Lydia are almost at the shelter. I should go."

Tess squeezed my hand. "I don't want anything to happen to you." She leaned over the table and pressed her lips to mine, then hurried away.

*****

I arrived at the shelter still smarting from Tess's departure and André's betrayal, imagining an emotional scene in which Alicia and Kizzy are reunited, two girls overjoyed to see each other, the scene inspired by my desire to feel good about something — anything.

I was surprised to see Clara in the company of Preacher Simmons. He smiled at me, then offered his hand.

"Hope there's no hard feelings. I was just trying to protect Alicia. Kinda said some things that weren't Christian like. Anyway, I come here today to make sure no one messes with her." He pulled back his shirt to reveal an automatic weapon tucked in his jeans. "The Lord works in mysterious ways, but sometimes it's best to have backup."

Lydia and Alicia joined us. The door of the house opened, and Rachael stepped out onto the porch. She surveyed the small gathering and shook her head. "I don't know what you all are doing here, but Kizzy isn't taking any visitors."

Alicia stepped forward. "I need to see her."

195

"No, girl, you don't," snapped Rachael. "Nothing good will come of it."

Kizzy appeared at the door, pushed past Rachael, and stopped only a few feet from Alicia. For a moment, Kizzy remained silent, her face distorted by anger.

"You said you would protect me!" she screamed through uncontrolled sobs. "You said we would start a new life together, but that was a lie, too! You don't care about anyone but yourself!"

Alicia stepped forward and reached for Kizzy's hand. "I didn't lie. I meant what I said. I'm sorry..."

Kizzy pushed her back. "You said I would be safe, but I'll never be safe. Never!"

Kizzy ran inside and slammed the door behind her.

"You got what you came for!" shouted Rachael. "Now leave us in peace."

Preacher Simmons tried to console Alicia, but she pushed him away. Lydia followed after her, leaving Tess, the preacher, Clara and me staring at the now empty porch.

"Children trying to protect children," said Preacher Simmons, shaking his head. "That's not what Jesus taught us."

"I don't know about what Jesus would say," said Clara, "but that man Giles deserves to rot in hell."

The preacher nodded in agreement. "If there's truly a God, it'll be soon."

I didn't say so, but I'd reached the same conclusion.

I walked slowly back to my car. The gloom that had gripped me most of the morning gave way to a moment of clarity. I had no money, no immediate source of income, and no house. Even my doubloons were lost somewhere in the pile of ash and broken glass that had been my house. I needed to determine if the house was insured, the cost of removing the debris, and my options in selling the land. I needed to return Karen's Amazon box to Clara. More importantly, I needed to find a job, or more accurately, a career. I also needed to find a way of caring for Ethy that didn't require living with her. Making a list of tasks was a welcome but temporary distraction from a question I couldn't answer but couldn't erase from my head: What was to become of Alicia and Giles?

CHAPTER TWENTY

I spent the rest of the morning searching the debris of my house for anything I might salvage. The exercise was pointless, and I knew it, but I had nothing pressing to do. To my surprise, I found a small metal box. While the paint had been turned to ash, the box appeared to be in good shape. I shook it and heard the clank of coins. Smiling, I opened it and gazed at the collection of doubloons that represented most of my remaining liquid assets. All, it seemed, was not lost.

I arrived at Ethy's house to find her sitting at the kitchen table with Lydia drinking coffee and smoking.

"I get one a day," said Ethy defensively. "It's not like I'm going to get lung cancer in the few years I have left."

I poured a cup of coffee but didn't join them at the table. "Tess went back to New York," I said.

Ethy slowly exhaled a cloud of smoke. "She told me this morning before you left. Coming here and watching how a real American family works probably made her think about what she'd be missing by rejecting Hank's proposal."

The comment was followed by a momentary silence, which gave way to peals of laughter.

"You probably scared that girl shitless," said Lydia.

Ethy laughed until she started coughing. "God knows what we are role models for, but family harmony ain't one of them."

"We do okay," I said.

Ethy cleared her throat. "We do, don't we?"

"That's not all the news," said Lydia. "Alicia packed her things and left. I thought she might, especially after Kizzy broke her heart."

"Since we're all in a sharing mood, André told me that he can't protect us after all. Basically, Giles will get the laptop back and come after us. I explained this to Alicia, which is probably why she bolted. She's in danger, and she has no money, unless she stole some from you before she left."

Ethy crushed her cigarette in an ashtray and lit another. "I wish I were surprised. That Giles man is going to ruin us all."

Lydia handed me a scrap of paper. "All of that might explain why Gwen Farrell called me a half hour ago, insisting on speaking with you about Alicia. Before you ask a lot of questions that I can't answer, call this number. She sounded pretty wound up. Could be the coke she snorts, but it might be something important."

I dialed the number. After one ring, I heard a barely audible voice: "Meet me at the front of the high school in twenty minutes. I think Alicia's going to kill Dillon. Hurry."

I slipped the phone back in my pocket.

"Well?" asked Ethy.

"For some reason, Gwen believes Alicia is going to kill Dillon Farrell. I'm supposed to meet her in twenty minutes. Unless, of course, I'm too busy."

"You have to hand it to the kid for being motivated," said Lydia. "Hope she shoots him in the nuts."

"You're not seriously thinking of letting a child commit murder?" asked Ethy.

"Dillon killed Megan," I said evenly. "Maybe we shouldn't interfere."

The room went silent. Ethy left the table and ran into the master bedroom.

"I didn't see that coming," said Lydia, "from Alicia or you. But you know she won't get close enough to shoot him before someone shoots her. Hell, even if she manages to whack the bastard, she'll be tried for murder. Florida likes to execute people. Giles would insist on it."

Ethy returned, a grim look on her face. "Maurice's gun is missing."

"Was it loaded?" I asked.

"A full clip."

Detective Murphy walked slowly into the room. "I'm a bit stoned, but I'm not deaf. You people have no clue what you're up against. I may not have much time left, but I'm going to see this case to its end." He turned to me. "I'm going with you. I don't have the strength to argue with you, so if you start in with the usual bullshit, I may just shoot you myself. Clear?"

I said it was. Perfectly.

*****

Key West High School is located east of the historic district. To reduce car traffic during Fantasy Fest Week, the school parking lot is repurposed as a shuttle lot. I paid the twenty-five dollars and walked with Detective Murphy to the front of the school. I had no idea what Gwen looked like, but I didn't have to. A small group of onlookers was pointing at her and taking photos.

True to Giles' preferences, Gwen was shapely, even if artificially so, with long hair and brown eyes. The curse of beauty was that it attracted predators before defenses could be learned. While her public persona was the beautiful wife of a famous and successful actor, I had no doubt that as a member of Giles' harem, her past was both tragic and painful.

"Thank you for coming," she said, her voice cracking. "We've got to stop her. I'm sure they'll kill her."

"Come with me," said Detective Murphy.

We followed him to the front of the school, where he flashed his badge at a policewoman positioned at the entrance door. He said something, then she moved aside.

"I told her Gwen had to use the bathroom," he said. "Now, let's back up. Tell me who you are, what you know, and how you know it."

Gwen wiped her eyes. "I'm married to Dillon Farrell, the actor. A few days ago, he and his friend Peter Cobb did something to Megan. I'm not sure…Megan is dead…"

She was crying uncontrollably, her body shaking. She slumped toward the floor, but Detective Murphy grabbed her arms and propped her up. "Listen to me. You need to get a grip if you want to save Alicia. What happened?"

The detective's stern voice calmed her. She wiped her eyes. "Dillon told Giles that Peter attacked Megan and killed her. Then Giles found out last night that Dillon sent Bruno to Fort Jefferson to find Alicia and get something she stole. He was really pissed off.

He got into it with Dillon, who tried to convince Giles he didn't know what Bruno was up to, but then Giles played a recording of Bruno saying Dillon was paying him. None of it makes sense to me, but I heard they found Bruno's body this morning. Then Alicia called me, wanting to go to Giles's party."

"What party?" I asked.

"Giles is throwing a party this afternoon before the grand Fantasy Fest parade. The party is for the people on the cruise and important people from everywhere abroad. Alicia called me and asked if could get her a costume — it's a gangster theme, like in the 1920s — and a ticket. I asked her if she thought Giles had forgiven her. She said everything was good. I thought it might be odd that she wanted to meet in town, but I did what she asked. Then she told me that Dillon had killed Megan. Nothing more than just a matter-of-fact statement that he killed her. But I could see it in her eyes. Alicia has always been aloof, but that look... I asked her again if she was okay. She just said that she felt safe...No. She said I'm going to feel safe. The whole conversation was like weird. After she left, I guess it sunk in that she might be planning to kill Dillon or Giles. They both have bodyguards. She tries anything, they won't hesitate to shoot her. You need to stop her."

She handed me an envelope. "Here are two tickets you can use to get into the party. Everyone there will be dressed like gangsters. You'll need costumes of some kind so no one notices you. I'm sure they'll check everyone at the door for weapons, so don't bother bringing guns. Just find her before she does something stupid."

We escorted Gwen to a waiting car. "Dillon is a pig," she said. "If he killed Megan, then he needs to pay. I get that. I just don't want Alicia to get hurt."

On the way back to Ethy's house, Detective Murphy and I

argued over who was going to the party and who wasn't. Even as we stepped inside the house, he continued to assert that he would be going. Lydia and Ethy took my side leaving the detective outnumbered. He played his trump card and the discussion ended.

"I am still a cop," he said. "The murder of Megan Jones is my case, and I will see it to its conclusion. Both Jake and I will attend the party. What we need are costumes."

"You can't go unarmed," said Lydia.

"That's why I need a hat," he said.

*****

Lydia and Ethy spent an hour in Ethy's garage looking through boxes and an assortment of trunks. "I never got around to donating Maurice's clothes to Goodwill," she said. "By the time the pain of his death faded, I'd just forgotten about them."

The search of the trunks produced a double-breasted jacket and a dark sport coat with wide white-chalk stripes. "Maurice thought he looked suave in these clothes. I mean, we didn't dress up too often, but when we to private parties, he liked to strut around in what he thought was high fashion. Honestly, I would have been embarrassed if anyone I cared about went to those parties, but for the most part I was spared the humiliation. Fortunately, they didn't have Facebook back then."

I combined the striped jackets with a pair of white chinos. For shoes, all I had were sneakers, but in a crowd, few people were going to pay much attention to my feet.

Detective Murphy donned the double-breasted jacket and what looked like a fedora and absolutely looked the part of a Prohibition-era gangster. He gave me the keys to his car and asked that I retrieve a black bag tucked behind the spare tire.

With Ethy, Lydia, and I watching, he opened the bag and started removing handguns. Soon, a small collection had been assembled and placed on the kitchen table. Then he pulled a small automatic and examined it. "This might work," he said.

He took off the hat and put the gun inside. "Not a lot of firepower, but a well-placed round will stop about anyone, or at least distract them. I just need some tape."

"How do you plan on getting that through security?" I asked.

"We have to hope that the security guys are using wands. No one ever wands your head. If they find it, I'll just tell them it's a joke — part of my costume."

He looked at his watch. "I'm going to lie down for thirty minutes. With the traffic, we'll need to get on the road then." He hefted the small gun and smiled. "You know, this could be fun."

I laughed. "Let's party."

CHAPTER TWENTY-ONE

The key to blending into a crowd is to look bored and boring. As it turned out, the pre-parade party-goers seemed to be competing for the most outrageous combination of zoot suits, feathered hats, flapper dresses, and Fedoras. Our costumes were plain and minimal, relegating us to visual background noise.

I had taken some comfort in Gwen's warning about security at the party. Alicia wasn't any more likely to get a gun into the ballroom than we were. Murphy wasn't happy about not having what he called a "real gun," even as I reminded him that our mission was to find Alicia and keep her from doing anything stupid.

Whatever security procedures had been planned quickly fell apart when the guests arrived *en masse*. The doors opened and hordes of gangsters and flappers flooded the entry, overwhelming men with wands and those trying to check purses. Many of the guests were carrying weapons as part of their costumes. Some were no doubt props. Others looked to be the real thing.

Confusion morphed to anger as the security crew attempted to confiscate guns from the wealthy (and deeply offended) party-goers. Murphy removed his hat and dropped it onto the floor near a screening table. The maneuver was odd, making me wonder if he'd had a stroke or otherwise lost his mind. When he stood up, he motioned for me to follow him inside. He pulled me aside and opened his hand, revealing a thirty-eight revolver. "Guy had it strapped to his ankle. Now I feel dressed."

"I'm happy for you. Now let's find Alicia and get out of here before you actually have to use it."

A man carrying a tray of coconut shrimp walked by. "We can eat while we look," he said, grabbing two shrimp and a napkin.

"Just keep your hat on and your face covered."

We stood together at the back of a grand ballroom. The room was arranged with tables toward the front and an open area at the back where we entered. An elevated platform had been erected at the front of the room to accommodate guests of honor. As the ballroom filled with bodies, a small band played jazz that sounded to my ear to be a little modern for Prohibition. Momentarily, I was lost in the wailing of a saxophone and had to fight the impulse to get closer to the source.

I walked through the tables looking for signs of Alicia while keeping my eyes open for Giles. I found him standing on the platform behind a large table, his arms folded Mussolini-style.

Seeing Giles Horan fully illuminated was underwhelming. For a man with a reputation for power and a penchant for beautiful women, he was strikingly homely. His body seemed to be made of leftover parts — arms from a short man, legs from someone of average height, and a head that had a lot in common with a basketball or a pumpkin.

What seemed to go unnoticed by the sycophants of the world was his penchant for young girls. When news broke that he was under investigation for multiple counts of sexual assault, the usual defenders of the media were the first to attack it. Even as more of his victims came forward, the very people who should have taken the side of the victims were silent, allowing his lawyers to attack his accusers as liars, whores, and drug addicts. When prosecutors allowed him to plead to a single count of soliciting sex, the foundations that loved his money forgave him and dozens of rich and powerful men, who had shared his stable of young and attractive girls, breathed a sigh of relief. Now they feasted on his caviar, fillet mignon, and expensive wine, indifferent to the plight of those he exploited.

*****

Watching Giles lord over men and women of power and wealth, smug and confident that he would never be asked to account for his crimes, sent me into a silent rage. Giles was soon joined by Dillon Farrell, who was dressed in a suit with wide lapels, broad stripes, and pleated pants. The two of them laughed and smiled, pretending not to notice being noticed.

With a room filled with would-be mobsters, a security crew of three stood out like clothed men at a nudist camp. The uniform of the security people seemed to be cargo shorts and floral shirts overlaid with shoulder holsters holding large automatic weapons. The firepower suggested that Giles had enemies, or at least thought he did, and wasn't taking any chances.

The joviality evaporated when Peter Cobb sprinted to the stage and headed straight for Dillon Farrell.

Murphy tapped my arm. "This can't be good."

We moved close enough to hear Peter's voice, but not so close as to be recognized. The first words I heard clearly were "fucking rat." He tossed the chair aside, then slammed a wine glass over

Dillon's head. Blood trickled down Dillon's forehand and dripped from Peter's hand. The audience watched the spectacle with an uncertain amusement. Laughter and even a spattering of applause could be heard from the onlookers. Given the theme of the party, they figured the episode was part of a skit. But when Peter grabbed a wine bottle and came at Dillon again, the snickers turned to groans.

Though the events unfolded in front of me, I am unsure what transpired next. Adrenaline can fog memory and distort details, and the normal rhythm of time is slowed, as if I am watching a film shot in slow motion. As I remember, this was the sequence of events:

While Peter was rushing toward Dillon, I caught a glimpse of Alicia as she glided toward the stage, a gun in her hand.

I moved toward her, reaching her as Peter raised the wine bottle into position to strike Dillon. Alicia's attention was focused on Giles, repeating the words, "I have to be free of him," softly but audibly. When I reached her, she began to sob. For a moment, she stared at me, pleading with her eyes. She didn't resist as I took the gun from her hand. She closed her eyes and slid to the floor. Detective Murphy was next to me, the thirty-eight he stole from the guard in his hand, screaming at me to get down.

One of the floral-shirted security guards fired at Peter. In a classic case of contagious shooting, the other guards drew their guns. A thunderous barrage of bullets ripped through the attorney general's son, the chairs on the stage, the dishware, and the wine glasses sending blood, shards of glass, and dust into the air.

Giles scurried away from Peter, running like a rat across the stage. I imagined him looking at me, smiling at me, daring me, then mocking me. I pointed the gun Alicia had stolen at Giles and willed my hand to be steady. My finger touched the trigger. I heard two shots, then I felt a searing jolt of pain just above my left ear.

Just as suddenly as the deafening din of gunfire had filled the room, all was silent. Smoke wafted across the room, Peter lay on the stage, his body pierced by a flurry of bullets. Dillon tried to stand, a cascade of blood covering his face, only to collapse into a pile of debris.

Sitting on a chair, his hand over his stomach, was Giles Horan. Blood leaked through his fingers. He looked puzzled, unaware perhaps that his life was trickling away.

I felt a hand on my shoulder. "Get her out of here," said Murphy removing the gun from my hand. "We'll clean this up. Go through the kitchen. You have to hurry before the building is sealed."

I grabbed Alicia's arm, but she wouldn't move. "He's dead, isn't he?" she said. "I killed him."

Murphy took her other arm and we lifted her to her feet. "He's dead, but no, sweetie, you didn't kill him," he said. "He was hit by a stray bullet. You didn't kill anyone." He looked at me. "Neither did you."

She stared blankly. "I couldn't live knowing he was going to come after me or Kizzy. I couldn't."

I gently pulled her toward the kitchen doors. "It's okay," I said. "He won't come after you or anyone else. We have to go."

Alicia stared at me. "You're bleeding."

"I'm fine."

"I know what you did."

I shook my head. "I didn't do anything. But even if I did, this is our secret. No one will know we were here. This is your chance to start over."

Detective Murphy handed me a napkin from a table. "You need to go."

211

As we entered the kitchen, she stepped in front of me. "I don't owe you anything."

"No. You don't."

"I can take care of myself." Tears streamed down her face. "I don't need you. I don't need anyone."

She pressed her face into my shoulder. "I've got no place to go. What am I going to do now?"

EPILOGUE

The shooting at the pre-parade gala was investigated by state, local, and federal agencies. Despite pages of testimony from eyewitnesses and bags of evidence taken from the scene, conclusions as to what happened and who did what to whom proved elusive. What was known for certain was that Peter Cobb, the son of the Attorney General of the United States, had attacked Dillon Farrell, a famous actor known for his portrayal of hero Mitch Westly, and that the attack triggered a response from armed security personnel.

Complicating matters was the fact that the three members of the security staff in attendance disappeared before the police were able to get from various Fantasy Fest venues to Giles Horan's private key. Alicia and I managed to board a shuttle going from the key to the mainland just before the island was locked down.

Several dozen bullets were found in the ballroom walls and furnishings. Much of what was recovered were fragments without any evidentiary value. Curiously, the few intact rounds that were found matched unregistered guns used in other crimes.

The bullet that killed Giles Horan was never definitively identified. The bullet entered his chest, nicked his aorta, then exited his back. The gun that fired it was thought to be a thirty-eight, the same caliber of gun stolen by Detective Murphy when we first entered the room. Another report listed the wound as being caused by a nine-millimeter automatic, which was the caliber of weapons used by several of the security guards and Maurice's automatic, the one I was holding when all hell broke loose. The police never recovered either weapon and never connected the shooting to either Detective Murphy or me.

Amid the chaos I remember pointing the gun in Giles' direction and hearing two shots, but cannot recall feeling the gun recoil. Given that Detective Murphy was close by, the sound I heard could have come from his weapon.

Giles had never been charged with a serious crime much less convicted of one. But by all accounts, he deserved to die. For most of his adult life he managed to live outside the rules that apply to everyone else, his power and money provided him with a shield of immunity from the consequences of his behavior within a justice system ill-equipped to handle individuals with leverage over those who are supposed to administer justice blindly.

So, while I believe in the concept of innocent until proven guilty, a trial by jury of one's peers and all of the other trappings of due process, I have come, albeit reluctantly, to accept that those precepts don't apply to someone who regards himself as above the law. Giles lived in a ruleless world and that's where he died. I may have been an unwitting participant in this extrajudicial process, but whoever shot Giles saved other girls and young women from the horrors experienced by Alicia and Megan. If this means that I have come to accept that cold-blooded vigilantism is justifiable, or at least easily rationalized, then so be it.

Detective Murphy managed to cast himself as a hero of sorts. He spun a tale about having learned from a credible source that

Dillon Farrell's life was in danger. Knowing that such rumors were common and not wanting to disrupt the festivities, he attended in costume and undercover. He was credited with reacting quickly to move guests to safety, thus avoiding additional loss of life.

Detective Murphy didn't live to hear the kind but inflated statements about his valor. He died two weeks later in a hospice surrounded by Ethy, Lydia, and me. He received an impressive funeral procession that included officers from the Keys, Palm Beach, and Miami police departments and a eulogy delivered by Roy Perching that was part fiction and part factual, although even the almost-true elements were products of Roy's selective memory. I hadn't known the detective long, but the funeral made me realize that I missed him.

Alicia stayed with us a few days, then disappeared. I learned later that some of Ethy's jewelry was missing too. Unbothered, Ethy said she never wore it anyway.

The police investigations that followed were hampered by the lack of an answer to a single question: Why did Peter Cobb assault Dillon Farrell, an actor who claimed they were mere acquaintances? Gwen, Dillon's wife, could have disputed Dillon's assertion, but didn't. Dillon offered no explanation other than to speculate that Peter was hopped up on drugs and thought Dillon was actually Mitch Westly, the character he played in the movies, and was playing out some drug-induced fantasy. The explanation made no sense, but the authorities seemed to accept it.

Shortly after Dillon's movie was released, she filed for divorce. Not only did Dillon not contest the divorce he also opted not to assert his rights under their prenup. While the settlement agreement wasn't made public, the numbers leaked to the media made it clear Gwen wouldn't have to worry about money ever again.

She soon disappeared from Florida but not from the tabloids. Stories suggesting a romantic connection between her and Peter Cobb got plastered onto front pages of all the grocery store tabloids, most likely written by Dillon's publicists. Those stories were quickly countered by headlines hinting that Peter's attack on Dillon was the result of a lover's quarrel, most likely contributed by creative writers working for Gwen.

Harold Cobb, the Attorney General of the United States and one-time employer of André Mitchell, also remained silent. I had no way of knowing if Harold had turned over the laptop to Giles before his death, but regardless, the AG knew that Dillon blamed Peter for the murder of Megan Jones. Of course, Harold couldn't come forward without revealing that he had knowledge of multiple crimes, including rape, murder, and sex-trafficking and that he had, by hiring André, participated in the crimes André committed.

Dillon recovered, albeit with a nasty scar on his forehead that threatened to drop him from the "handsomest man in Hollywood" list.

Megan Jones' murder was never associated with the party shootings and her case remained closed. According to the official record, her life was erased from the earth by an accident.

Giles' death created a windfall in business for lawyers all over the country. Women claiming to be victims filed lawsuits against Giles' estate asserting claims for damages from his actions, some of which were decades old. While the media focused on the salacious details of Giles' sexual appetites, some major law firms quietly filed motions to seal records that might otherwise be produced in the discovery process. The motions themselves were sealed, but the implication was that some of Giles' friends feared him as much in death as they did when he was alive.

A few months after Detective Murphy's funeral, I received a text from Lydia that included a photograph of Alicia sitting at a computer: "Murphy left the bulk of his estate to me with instructions to do what I could for Alicia. After a rough start, counseling, and the usual negotiations, she is now enrolled in an online course to get a high school diploma. She's also taking piano and singing lessons. She'd say hello but she's afraid you'd say 'I told you so.' She asked if you and Tess had ever gotten together. Best, Lydia."

Tess first heard about the shoot-out from Ethy. I had been admitted to the hospital for observation. Ethy made the mistake of answering my phone and explaining that I couldn't talk because I'd been shot. Tess asked too many questions for Ethy, who decided that putting that horse back into the barn was more than she could handle. She passed me the phone, saying that Tess was upset about something but wasn't speaking clearly.

"What the hell were you thinking getting involved in a gun fight with Giles?"

I heard Hank's voice urging her to finish the call - a request that temporarily redirected her ire from me to him.

"It wasn't like that," I said. "Alicia went to a Giles party with the intention of shooting Dillon Farrell."

"What party? You're not making any sense. You were shot?"

"Technically. Peter Cobb was shot a few times and died. Giles was hit once and he's dead, too. I was hit by a bullet fragment and just needed a few stitches. All in all, it was a pretty successful afternoon. How are you doing?"

"You're the dumbest man I've ever met."

"I don't think you're giving Hank enough credit," I managed to counter.

"You stupid…" Snickering precluded her from saying more. "That's not funny."

"I've got a nurse who's got what looks like a needle and sutures. I'm good. You take care."

After Detective Murphy's funeral, Ethy and I agreed that I should take the job with ClearSeas. The job required that I spend part of the year on a boat. Actually, it didn't, but I insisted that my duties be broadened to include time on the research vessels collecting the data I was hired to analyze. I rented a small furnished condo in Miami close to the ClearSeas' office and made plans to move in at the beginning of December.

I used the month of November to find care for Ethy and to deal with what was left of my house. As it turned out, the house wasn't insured, but with the house gone, the whole property was actually worth more. I sold the lot and put the proceeds in the bank.

I had always been told that my mother had inherited the house from her parents and then passed it on to me. At closing, I learned that my mother had actually purchased the house just after arriving in Key West in 1990. Even more surprising was that she had paid cash. Ethy was equally surprised, leaving us both to wonder where my mother had come from and where she'd gotten the money.

Shortly before I left, Ethy took me aside and asked me if I'd thought any more about the emails exchanged between my mother and the man named James. The short answer was yes, but with Ethy, my answering in the affirmative naturally required a long explanation. I told her I knew he loved my mother, and that I wasn't conceived in some drunken fit, which was comforting. I also admitted that while I had a certain level of curiosity about my biological father, I realized my adoptive parents truly loved me, Maurice was as a good a father as I could have wanted, and Ethy had a unique approach to mothering which I learned to appreciate.

To my relief, I was spared any further discussion about my intentions regarding finding my father and my mother's killer. I'm not sure what I would have said if asked. I read the email correspondence between them almost every day, hoping to fill a void that is bottomless. Of course, I knew that the handful of emails was never going to answer the questions that dogged me day and night.

The day I headed to Miami, after Ethy and I had said all the goodbyes we could muster, she looked at me with tears in her eyes. "Your father's name is James Martin. I should have told you about him, but the truth is that I was afraid of losing you. I still am."

Ethy wrapped her arms around me and sobbed on my shoulder. "That will never happen," I said patting her on the back. We parted, and I drove off realizing that Ethy had just given me a key to unlocking my past.

Not all loose ends were cleaned up the way I anticipated. When Harold Cobb announced his candidacy for President, I could barely contain my anger. A month later, an article appeared in the New York Times about a video depicting the murder of a young girl. The article didn't mention Peter Cobb or Dillon Farrell, but someone had leaked the fact that the video of Megan's murder existed and that Harold Cobb knew about it and had suppressed it.

The next day, I got a text message from a number I didn't recognize that read simply: "Some messes take longer to clean up than others." I wasn't sure what had provoked André to reveal the video, but soon thereafter, Harold Cobb not only withdrew his presidential candidacy but resigned as Attorney General.

Tess didn't marry Hank. She also didn't come looking for me, at least not right away. After Christmas, I started receiving text messages from her that contained only photographs. Africa was first, followed by a series of shots showing penguins in Antarctica.

A text I received last week, however, sparked my interest. "Do you know anyone who could show me a lionfish?"

I did, and I said so.

Continue reading for a preview of

The Gene Police

By

Elliott Light

THE GENE
POLICE

ELLIOTT LIGHT

PROLOGUE

I live with four cats on what was once a poor farm outside the small town of Lyle, Virginia. I share a small suite of offices with an attorney named Robbie Owens in a renovated townhouse on the north end of town and spend most of my days in my office managing the estate of Reilly Heartwood, a famous country singer and my biological father. He was a generous man who left me a lot of money, what was once a poor farm, a mansion on the edge of town, responsibility for four elderly people who once lived on the poor farm but currently live in the mansion, and a maze of tax problems stemming from his donations to charities that had lost their 501(c)(3) status.

Reilly Heartwood, who performed under the name of CC Hollinger, died without telling me what our relationship was. My mother, to hide the shame of being pregnant with me, had married a nice but formal man named William Harrington and told me that he was my father. William, who stuck me with the preposterous name, "J. Shepard Harrington," neither played with me nor taught me what sons are supposed to learn from their dads. I guess he was nice to my mother in an old school way, but he wasn't pleased when my mother took to calling me Shep. He traveled a lot, so I wasn't surprised when one morning he wasn't there for breakfast.

After a few days, I asked my mother if he was coming back, and she just said, "no." We never spoke of him again.

I am an attorney with expertise in corporate and commercial matters and a smattering of civil law issues. My limited knowledge of criminal law was acquired when I was prosecuted by the federal government for criminal fraud and sentenced to prison. I served three years before the legal system finally acknowledged, albeit reluctantly, that I wasn't guilty.

The experience exposed a system designed to value conviction rates over truth - a system that regards sentences as final and irrevocable. For me, the most important lesson learned was that it's far easier for an innocent person to get into prison than out.

I was released from prison in time to watch my mother die of cancer. Less than a year later, I came to Lyle to deal with Reilly's untimely death from a gunshot wound initially reported as self-inflicted. I insisted that he wouldn't have killed himself and, in fact, proved that he'd been murdered. That's when I learned he was my father. While poking my nose into Reilly's death, I also learned what it was like to be shot. Having been shot once, you might think I wouldn't get involved in another murder investigation. But last summer, I was drawn into the murder of a woman who worked at a research facility that used chimpanzees as test subjects. Sydney Vail, who was later accused of the crime, brought me a stolen chimp named Kikora. Defending Sydney and Kikora was legally challenging, not to mention painful. I was shot for the second time, an experience that would make a rational lawyer think twice before getting involved in a third murder.

While not wanting to sound defensive, I did think twice - actually more than twice - about getting involved in the murder case of Jennifer Rice. I set boundaries to avoid being drawn in too

224

deeply. I agreed to help around the edges of the case. My good intentions, however, were undone by an overdeveloped aversion to people who believe they can hurt others and get away with it. So while I denied that I was trying to find out who killed Jennifer Rice, I was wondering who did.

Jennifer Rice was in her late seventies when she was beaten to death. Although she was famous for her travel books and photographic essays, I had never heard of her until Reggie Mason appeared in my office to ask a favor. Reggie is a black state trooper whom I met while working the Sydney Vail case. He is a large, bear-like man in his early forties. To some, he appears intimidating, but he is one of the gentlest men I've ever known.

I hadn't seen Reggie Mason for several months when he arrived at my office on a cold February day in 2002. Perhaps his arrival alone should have alerted me to the import of his visit. Certainly I should have read the cues on his face to know that his visit wasn't personal. Any misconceptions were quickly dispelled when Reggie announced that he needed to confess to various crimes and wanted my advice on how he should proceed.

Reggie's announcement certainly defined his future. He told a simple story of what he did and why. Because his actions constituted crimes under Virginia statutes, his future was in the hands of the power brokers of the legal system: the police, a prosecutor, and a judge. He asked me and my law partner, Robbie, to help him decide when and how to admit to his wrongdoing.

Yet, his announcement actually told volumes about the past - a past that none of us knew anything about, and one that would soon appear one painful revelation at a time.

CHAPTER ONE

Monday, February 11

The morning started innocently enough. Robbie was in her office talking to a client about a fence that had been installed on the client's property by the client's neighbor. I was working on a spreadsheet of Reilly's charitable deductions going back fifteen years in preparation for turning over Reilly's tax issues to a tax attorney.

My door was open, giving me a view of our small waiting room and the front door. My attention alternated from my computer screen to a large icicle hanging menacingly over the waiting room window. The icicle refracted the sunlight into a small swath of colors that flickered on the carpet. Objectively, this light display was not terribly exciting, but when compared to the unrelenting boredom of tax documents, the colors were fascinating.

The spell of the lights was broken when the door to the office was thrown open, allowing a surge of cold air to rush in. A moment later, the doorway was all but filled by the frame of Reggie Mason. He hesitated for a moment, then stepped inside and removed his dark glasses, his face expressionless while his eyes adjusted to the light. As I stood up, he saw me and flashed a smile.

"Hey, Shep. You got a minute?"

"What the hell are you doing here?" I offered him a hand, but he wrapped his arms around me and gave me a man-hug. When I stepped back I saw weariness and angst written on his face.

The door to Robbie's office opened and her client stepped out. The client was a small white woman, and she seemed to step back at the sight of a large black man. But he nodded his head, said "'ma'am" in a soft, southern voice, and she erupted in a smile. Reggie had that effect on people.

Robbie walked the client to the door and returned with a scowl on her face.

"It's good to see you, Reggie," she said firmly, "but I can't remember the arrival of an uninvited visitor, especially a cop, that wasn't made memorable by bad news."

Reggie shrugged. "Whether news is bad or good kind of depends on your perspective. I just need a favor."

"Why does the word 'just' always precede a request that smart people would say no to?" she asked.

Reggie forced another smile. "Maybe you'll say no. Maybe you won't."

"I'm sorry, Reggie, but men in general are untrustworthy. Cops and ex-felons even more so," Robbie said. "You've got a folder in your hand, so pardon me if I don't believe you're here to use the bathroom."

I am technically not an ex-felon. Robbie knows this but uses the reference when she's annoyed with me. From her tone, she suspected that Reggie and I were up to something that would distract me from my estate work. I decided it was best to allow her to negotiate with Reggie, but after two months of looking at tax records, I admit to being intrigued by what was in the folder he carried.

"All I want is a few minutes of your time," pressed Reggie. "After that, you can just say no. I hope you won't, but no hard feelings if you do."

Robbie led us into our small conference room. Pulling back a chair, she said, "You are going to explain why you're here, and then I'm going to explain how Shep has a meeting with an IRS agent in two weeks and can't be distracted until the audit is over."

Reggie took a seat. "It's just a small favor."

Robbie and I sat across from him. "What favor and how small?" she asked sternly.

Reggie opened the file and removed a stack of photographs. "Look at these and then I'll tell you what I need."

Robbie and I stared at a series of sweeping views of a pasture brimming with wild flowers. A farmhouse rose in the distance, a curl of smoke coming from its chimney. The photos were oddly familiar. A moment later, we stared at a close-up of the farmhouse that is now my current residence. The next picture stunned us both.

"Oh my God!" exclaimed Robbie. "That's Carrie! She can't be much older than we are now. She's so cute!"

In the next photo, two teenage boys with hardened, muscular bodies were leaning over a fence. "I think that's Harry and Cecil Drake," I said.

"No way," said Robbie excitedly. "Look at them. They're just kids."

I handed her a picture of a tall, thin man in his twenties standing on the porch and holding a cat. "That is Jamie Wren." Jamie Wren is now confined to a wheelchair and has trouble speaking.

The four of them - Carrie, Harry, Cecil, and Jamie—live in the mansion I inherited from Reilly Heartwood and are affectionately known as the "Residents." Cecil and Harry are now in their sixties, Jamie a little north or south of seventy, and Carrie over eighty.

We continued to shuffle through pictures of men and women that we didn't recognize. "Who took these and where did you get them?" asked Robbie.

"I don't know who took them," said Reggie. "But I thought you might ask the folks that used to live on your farm if they know. It would help me a lot."

"Help with what?" I asked.

"Just something I'm looking into," he said.

Robbie tossed the pictures onto the table. "That seems like a small enough favor, but there's no way we are going to help you look into something without knowing what it is. If this were official, you wouldn't be here. That may sound distrustful, but we need to protect our law licenses. Where were the pictures found and what are you looking into?"

Reggie looked at me. "Is she always like this?"

I nodded. "She is, but she's also right."

"I believe I'm guilty of illegal use of the state DNA databases and maybe a few more felonies. I'm trying to decide whether to turn myself in. Finding out who took the pictures of the poor farm might help."

I glanced at my friend, his usual happy demeanor replaced by a defiant gaze tinged with fear. Robbie looked at me, her distrustful attitude receding under the weight of Reggie's words.

"Give me a dollar," I said. Reggie returned a puzzled look. "We need to establish attorney client privilege."

Reggie handed me a ten. "I need that for lunch."

"Okay. Let's start at the beginning."

"Hold on," said Robbie. "We're not criminal attorneys. I don't know that we can provide you the kind of representation you need."

"I know that," replied Reggie. "But I trust you. That's the most important thing."

"Start by explaining why you were playing with DNA databases," I said.

Reggie hesitated, glanced at Robbie, then said, "It involves a murder."

I heard Robbie take a quick breath. "And you didn't mention this because…?"

"Because you might think I'm asking Shep to investigate the murder, and I'm not."

Robbie took Reggie's hand. "Now I'm completely lost. You want us to find someone who took photographs at the poor farm fifty years ago because that will help you solve a murder?"

Reggie shook his head. "No. Well, kind of maybe."

"One more time," I said, "and this time start at the beginning."

Reggie nodded and took a deep breath. "I was raised by my Aunt Betty after my parents were killed in a traffic accident. I was sixteen and she was forty-six. My Uncle Carl was in prison for armed robbery. Aunt Betty didn't have children, so she spoiled me a bit. When I entered the police academy, she told me that in 1953 she went to Sweetwater Hospital and gave birth to a baby boy named John Mason Langard. Sweetwater accepted black patients, so her race shouldn't have been a problem."

"But it was," offered Robbie.

"That's not it," replied Reggie. "Aunt Betty was told that the

231

baby died of a heart defect, and that she had complications during childbirth that left her unable to have any more kids. Aunt Betty didn't believe the story they told her about Baby John and asked me to find out what really happened. To make her feel better, I said I would. I thought that would end it. But she kept asking me if I'd learned anything. I didn't have the courage to tell her that I had no idea how to investigate his death. I guess she thought that since I'd become a cop, I could just go into some file and look it up."

"What did she think happened to Baby John?" I asked.

"Either he was given away or he was murdered."

Robbie shook her head. "You don't believe that, do you?"

"I didn't at first," said Reggie, "but when you've heard the whole story, you can decide for yourself. So, Virginia was one of the first states to maintain a DNA database of felons. I became a trainer in the use of the database. I selected my uncle's DNA profile as a training tool. With each class, I ran his DNA against new samples entered into the database, hoping to find a partial match in the database that I could use to determine if Baby John was still alive.

"To be clear, the odds of this working were very small. The DNA used in criminal investigations is not particularly useful for establishing family connections. I had my aunt's DNA profile, so I had a pretty good idea of what my cousin's profile would look like. Even so, for me to find him, he would've had to have been at a crime scene in Virginia where DNA samples were taken, or he would've had to have been accused of committing a serious crime. I did this for ten years just so I could tell my aunt that I hadn't given up.

"And then last month, the system provided a sample that statistically had a high probability of being the offspring of my aunt and uncle. I didn't believe it would ever happen, but there it was. The sample was taken from the house of a murdered woman. The murder victim was an elderly white female named Jennifer Rice."

I was eager to learn more about the murder, but Robbie cut me off.

"Why would the hospital lie about your cousin dying?" asked Robbie.

"I don't know," replied Reggie. "But using the DNA database for personal reasons is a felony."

"I'm not sure if your conduct was actually criminal," I said. "I mean, you were authorized to access the database for training purposes. I don't see the point in telling anyone, particularly since you used the data you acquired for a legitimate purpose."

"The thing is, officially, my uncle had no children, so there is no reason for the investigators of Jennifer Rice's murder to look at DNA profiles in which some, but not all, of the loci match. I haven't told them about Baby John, so I'm probably obstructing a police investigation, which I suppose is another crime."

"What does any of this have to do with the pictures of the poor farm?" pressed Robbie.

Reggie handed us one more photo. Robbie and I studied it, unsure for a moment what we were looking at. The picture was back-lit. In the foreground, intentionally underexposed, was the silhouette of a woman. She appeared to be holding something against her chest.

Robbie took a sudden breath. "It's a baby!"

Reggie nodded. "That picture was taken at Shep's farm fifty years ago."

"You think it's your cousin?" I asked.

233

"Of course I do, but rationally it could be anyone's baby. It may be white or it may be black. I think the woman is white but I can't be sure. But it's all I have. If I can find the person who took the pictures, I might be able to find my nephew. In case I'm charged and arrested, I need to track him down before I confess to anything. I also need to know what he was doing at the scene of a murder."

"Okay," I said. "I get that you want to find who took the pictures and find your cousin. But let's talk about you confessing to what might be technical violations of the penal code. You know that's a bad idea."

Reggie leaned back in his chair. "I'm sure it is, but I'm kind of in a pickle."

"Explain pickle," said Robbie.

Reggie nodded. "The victim, Jennifer Rice, was seventy-eight when she was beaten to death in her home in Winchester. Detective Darnel Hunter is in charge of the investigation. The evidence points to a handyman named Albert Loftus. The case against Albert looks solid. They found a few pieces of Ms. Rice's jewelry in Albert's truck. Albert's story is what you might expect. He said he came to the house to clear the gutters of ice. He knocked and went inside to hook up a hose to the hot water heater. The door wasn't locked, which he says wasn't unusual. When he called out, Jennifer didn't answer. He saw a dark liquid on the tile floor in the living room, and followed a blood trail to the bedroom, where he saw Ms. Rice lying on the bed. She was covered with blood and badly beaten. He said he panicked and ran out. He didn't call the cops because he says they don't like him. He's found Jesus and given up his bad ways. Despite the jewelry found in his truck, he says he didn't steal anything and never touched her."

"What put the police on to Albert in the first place?" I asked.

"An anonymous tip."

"A little convenient," said Robbie, "but he had her jewelry."

"He did," agreed Reggie, "but I'm not sure he killed her, and neither is Detective Hunter."

"Based on what?" asked Robbie.

Reggie shrugged. "It doesn't feel right"

"What do you mean?" I asked.

"At worst, Albert's a petty thief, but he's not violent. No one is considering any other possibilities because they have no reason to. If I come forward with what I've learned, Albert at least get's a fair shake."

"And you open yourself up to being prosecuted," I said. "But if Albert's guilty, then your concealing the information about Baby John would have no impact on the investigation and you would have confessed for no reason other than to clear your conscience."

Reggie nodded. "That's the 'if' I've been grappling with. I don't know what Detective Hunter would do with the information if I gave it to her. And if Albert's not guilty, then my cousin's DNA is certainly material to the case. He could be a person of interest. Of course, if I were to cause my missing cousin to be investigated for murder, my Aunt Betty would never speak to me again."

I pointed at the folder. "What else do you have?"

"Nothing you need to know about," replied Reggie. "Humor me."

Reggie opened the folder. "I don't have the full case file, but a friend of mine who logs in the evidence at the Winchester police department sent me these." He placed a stack of photos on the table. "These are photos of Germany after World War II that were found in Jennifer's house. We've determined that they were taken by a Seymour Van Dyke. They look to be original prints, so I'm guessing she knew him. I checked and he was pretty famous in those days. A lot of what he took was published in Life Magazine and in the major newspapers. The first few are pretty hard to look at."

Reggie placed another stack of pictures next to the first. "These are travel photos that the victim took."

Robbie and I flipped through a dozen pictures of concentration camp victims, orphaned children, and starving animals. The black and white photos were somber and reflective. The color photos were striking; in each, the central horror was framed by something normal – a flower, an aid worker's bright dress, a group of vigorous soldiers playing baseball. In one picture, a small boy sat on a pile of human bones holding a sign in German. When I showed it to Reggie, he grimaced.

"I'm told it says, 'Are my parents in here?' That's tough to get your head wrapped around."

A second group of pictures depicted harbors, beaches, streams flowing through forests, and ancient ruins. These, too, were framed with a flair for the artistic.

"Jennifer Rice took some very nice pictures," said Robbie.

Reggie nodded. "In the early fifties, she was modestly successful at selling stories about the war, mostly about the way refugees were treated. But when the public's interest in war journalism faded, she turned her attention to travel pieces and published a number of very successful guide books. The books were illustrated with pictures she'd taken of people and places she'd encountered on her travels. Her photos were published as coffee table books. The travel and photo books made her quite wealthy. But we're getting off track. The police don't care about photographs. I only care about the pictures taken at the poor farm."

I handed the photos back to Reggie. "Let me see if I have this straight. All you want us to do is to ask the Residents if they remember anyone taking pictures at the poor farm or if they saw a woman with a baby"

"That's all," replied Reggie.

"What if Jennifer Rice took the pictures of the poor farm?" asked Robbie. "What if she was the one with the baby?"

Reggie shook his head. "I don't know. I just need to understand why my cousin's DNA was found at the house where she died. Where that leads is anyone's guess."

We sat quietly for a moment.

"What a mess," said Robbie. She glanced at me, then at Reggie. "I think we can ask a few questions."

I can't explain why those words excited me, but I did my best not to show it.

With the favor asked and granted, Reggie stood up. "Thank you. Some police reports, the photographs, and a CD of scanned versions are in the folder."

"Promise me you won't speak with Detective Hunter or the prosecutor without speaking with us first," I said.

Reggie agreed and left.

Robbie was quiet for a few moments, her attention focused again on the pictures. She showed me the photo of the boy on the pile of bones. "Can you, for an instant, imagine what that was like? I can't. I can't imagine people doing this to other people." She shook her head. "You can't help but wonder why more wasn't done to stop it." She picked up the photograph of the woman with

237

the baby. "Why would the hospital tell Reggie's aunt that her baby died if he didn't?"

"It's a mystery," I said.

"You don't think his cousin was actually murdered?"

I shrugged. "I have no reason to think so. If you're asking me if I believe that something like that might have happened, my answer is yes. The history we're taught was written by our parents and grandparents, all of whom were white. I doubt they were keen on sharing their generation's dirty laundry with their kids."

"Sounds like something you learned in prison," she said.

"Three years of mostly free time surrounded by some smart, educated inmates can open your eyes to the way the world is," I said.

Robbie grimaced, then tossed the pictures on the table. "I know you're worried about Reggie. But you can't get caught up in the murder of that woman. You just can't. I don't want you to, and none of your friends want you to. We can talk to the Residents about the pictures, see what they remember, and tell Reggie what we learn. I don't see how that can hurt anything, but that's all."

I smiled at her. "No," I said confidently. "That can't hurt."

The Gene Police

Available on AMAZON Today!

ABOUT THE AUTHOR

Elliott D. Light
www.elliottlight.com

Elliott Light grew up outside Washington, D.C. in McLean, Virginia before the beltway encircled the capital city, before farms were turned into housing developments, and before open fields became mega-malls.

Light attended the University of Virginia, receiving degrees in Electrical Engineering and Law. He has several patents to his name.

After stints as an environmental lawyer and a high tech in-house counsel, he practiced patent law in a private law firm.

Now retired, he resides in Naples, FL with his wife, Sonya. Throwaways is his fourth published novel.

OTHER BOOKS BY THIS AUTHOR

Shep Harrington Smalltown Mysteries

Lonesome Song - Book 1

Chain Thinking - Book 2

The Gene Police - Book 3

THROWAWAYS

CPSIA information can be obtained
at www.ICGtesting.com
Printed in the USA
FSHW020140231120
76040FS

9 781610 885287